TO KILL UPON A KISS

A DEAD COLD MYSTERY

BLAKE BANNER

RIGHTHOUSE

ISBN-13: 978-1-63696-009-8

ISBN-10: 1-63696-009-X

Cover design by: Damonza

Printed in the United States of America

www.righthouse.com

www.instagram.com/righthousebooks

www.facebook.com/righthousebooks

twitter.com/righthousebooks

PRAISE FOR THE DEAD COLD SERIES

Here are some of the over 100,000 five star reviews left for the Dead Cold Mystery series.

"Rex Stout and Michael Connelly have spawned a protege."

AMAZON REVIEW

"So begins one damned fine read."

AMAZON REVIEW

"Mystery that's more brain than brawn."

AMAZON REVIEW

"I read so many of this genre...and ever so often I strike gold!"

AMAZON REVIEW

"This book is filled with action, intrigue, espionage, and everything else lovers of a good thriller want."

AMAZON REVIEW

DEAD COLD MYSTERY SERIES

ONE

"Do you know how many times I have stood at this breakfast bar watching you cook bacon and eggs, wanting to tell you how much I love you when you cook bacon and eggs?"

It was seven o'clock in the morning and the smell of bacon and coffee was strong and rich on the air. She didn't look at me, but I could tell she was smiling. She said, "Yup."

"How many?"

She wielded the spatula with dazzling skill and slipped two eggs onto each plate as though it was easy. "I'm not going to tell you because then we'll get all mushy and we'll have to go upstairs and shower again. Put these on the table."

I carried the plates to the table with a self-satisfied saunter and a slightly foolish grin on my face. I sat, and as I reached out to pour the coffee, I felt her breath and her lips on my ear as she whispered in a husky growl, "Why d'you think I did it, dumbass?"

We were rescued from having to rush back to the shower by the jangling of my cell phone.

"Stone," I croaked. She grinned and sat.

"Good morning, John, it's John here."

I frowned, then my head cleared. "Oh, Inspector, good morning."

"Good morning. I'm sorry to call so early. I'm probably interrupting your breakfast. Look, I have a letter here, maybe nothing, but you never know, do you . . . ?"

I waited. He waited. I said, "No, Inspector, I guess you don't. What is the letter about?"

"The Westchester Angel."

I groped my way through the fog of coffee, bacon, and Dehan toward a dim glimmer of recollection. "Jane Doe, spring 2016, they found her body by the Westchester Creek. Raped and strangled."

Dehan was chewing, watching me with narrowed eyes, nodding slowly. Inspector Newman continued. "Probably raped, that's the one. Indeed. The writer claims to have information relevant to the case, and as the case has gone cold, I thought perhaps you would like to talk to him."

"Sure, of course. Give me his number. We'll give him a call and drop by . . ."

"Well, here's the thing. I've made an appointment for you to go and see him, this morning at nine, hence the early call."

"An appointment . . ."

I frowned. Dehan frowned in sympathy, sipping black coffee from her white cup.

"Yes, he's at Rikers, serving five years for possession of cocaine. His name is Wayne Harris. You can collect the file on your way. It's waiting on your desk."

"Thank you, sir . . ."

"See me when you get back. Let me know what he says."

"Yes, sir, we'll do that, as soon as we get back."

"Good. Nice talking to you. Enjoy your breakfast, John. And, uh, catch you later!"

I could hear the smile in his voice. I said, "Yes, sir, catch you later too . . ." But he'd already hung up.

———

It is a pretty roundabout route to Rikers Island from Morris Park, involving Randalls Island, the Robert F. Kennedy Bridge twice over water, and the Francis R. Buono Memorial Bridge just once. On the way we collected the file on the Westchester Angel case and Dehan read out loud while I drove. She had the window down, and the late May sun bathed her face as she raised her voice above the battering air and the growl of the Jaguar.

"Exactly a year ago, almost to the day. Monday the sixteenth of May, 2016, a body was found on an area of wasteland that runs for about half a mile along the west bank of the Westchester Creek. It was spotted by an employee at the quarry opposite the FedEx depot, who called 911."

I frowned. "Where was the body?"

She studied the file a minute, holding the pages between her fingers like a cigarette, to stop them flapping. After a moment she said, "Yeah. Zerega Avenue?" She glanced at me and I nodded. "You got the FedEx depot, the Golden Mango warehouse, and the quarry. There's a big patch of trees and rocks right on the river. She was down there." She carried on reading aloud. "Time of death was impossible to establish, as always. She'd been lying out in the open by the side of the river and lividity was advanced, though decay was still only in the initial stages. It was estimated that death occurred at some time between Saturday afternoon, when the guys from the quarry would likely have spotted her if she had been there, and the small hours of Sunday night to Monday morning."

We were crossing the first portion of the Robert F. Kennedy Bridge onto Randalls Island. I asked, "Cause of death was strangulation, right?"

She nodded, chewing her lip. "Mm-hm. She had some bruising to the face, especially the mouth, consistent with having been slapped hard or punched. ME suggested whoever hit her was big, or at least had large hands. Her wrists had been bound very tight with a silk handkerchief . . ." She looked at the photos and made a face. "But not like you'd expect. It was more like the old-fashioned cuffs. Like"—she held out her wrists to demonstrate—"he tied one wrist tight, then left some slack and tied the other wrist, so there was some play. Like he wanted her hands to have a certain amount of freedom." She shrugged. "Cause of death was strangulation. There was extensive bruising to the neck, the windpipe had been severely crushed, and the pattern of the bruises suggested that was done with the thumbs. No prints were recovered, so the killer probably used gloves."

My frown deepened as we passed over the sports fields and began to cross the water toward Astoria Park. "How was she lying?"

"Facedown, half in the water. Postmortem found that she'd had sex, so she may have been raped, premortem, perimortem, or postmortem. The semen was too decayed to provide a DNA profile."

I grunted. "Odd."

"What is?" Before I could answer, she said, "If she was raped Saturday night, say eight or nine o'clock, she could have been lying there about forty-eight hours, half in the water. The semen could well have decayed in that time."

I nodded, but I didn't say anything.

We crossed the long bridge over almost a mile of water, and she read me the last part of the file, about why Detective Ibanez had not been able to close the case. The victim had had no purse, no driver's license, no ID on her. There were no witnesses and her DNA and prints had got no hits on CODIS or IAFIS. All they had was the fact that she was Hispanic, in her early to midtwenties, and had a rather beautiful, expensive crucifix around her neck, inscribed with the name "Angela" on the back. Her clothes—a white blouse and a gray skirt—were good quality but modest and demure. The two latter facts had earned her the name the Angel of Westchester Creek in the more sensationalist press.

Three quarters of an hour later we were sitting in an interview room looking at the photos of the crime scene while we waited for Wayne Harris to be brought in. "I need to see it," I said.

Dehan nodded. "There are a couple of things I don't get . . ."

I agreed, but before I could say so there was a loud clang and the steel door rolled back. Two uniformed guards led in a tall man in an orange jumpsuit. He had the look and build of a quarterback: about six foot five, and I estimated his weight at about two hundred and thirty or forty pounds of solid muscle. He had a face that looked hard and solid too, with short hair, a square, raw concrete jaw, and a small, thin, cruel mouth that seemed permanently fixed in a thin, cruel smile. He had small, pale blue eyes, which he used now to observe Dehan as though he was calculating her size, weight, and intelligence.

The guards sat him in the chair opposite us and cuffed him to a metal ring on the table. One of them, a beefy black guy with humorous eyes, said, "If he gives you any trouble, you jess shout. We're right outside."

I thanked him, and they strolled out and clanged the door shut behind them. Wayne didn't look at me. He kept his eyes on Dehan. When he spoke, it was like sandpaper being dragged over twenty years' accumulated deposits of hardened nicotine in his throat.

"It's sure nice to talk to somebody who ain't a con. You ain't a con, are you, Detective?"

I said, "I'm Detective Stone, this is Detective Dehan. We're from the cold-cases unit at the Forty-Third Precinct. I was told you had some information for us."

He kept staring at Dehan, smiling, then slowly shifted his gaze to look at me. "Well, that all depends, Detective Stone of the Forty-Third Precinct. See, we are in the age of the Information Revolution. That may be something you don't fully appreciate, on account of your age. But Detective Dehan here, I figure she is closer to my age. Am I right, Detective Dehan? I figure maybe you will have a better understanding of what I am talking about. Information is where it's at. It's the name of the game."

Dehan raised an eyebrow at him that could have sliced the balls off a brass monkey.

I smiled and said, "If you're looking to sell information, Wayne, however old I may be, you need to talk to me. I run the cold-cases unit."

He still didn't look at me. He frowned and smiled simultaneously at Dehan and said, "Ouch! Male chauvinism strikes again. The white male still running the show, huh?"

I stood. "When you're ready to talk to me, Wayne, call the precinct. Right now you've got time to waste; we haven't."

Dehan stood.

Wayne sighed. "Take it easy, man! Take some time out from being you, we'd all be grateful." He grinned. "You feel me? Know what I'm sayin'?"

I waited, watching him. "Have you got something for me?"

"Yeah, man! Siddown, I got something for you."

I sat. Dehan went and stood in the corner, behind me, leaning against the wall with her arms crossed. I smiled to myself. She knew he wanted to play games with her, so she'd gone where she could observe him without distracting him. Now he was looking for her with his eyes.

I said, "You know something about the Westchester Creek murder in May 2016?"

He looked pained and gestured toward Dehan. "C'mon, man. She don't have to go away."

I leaned forward. "Okay, Wayne, this is your second warning. There won't be another. I think you're bored and you want to play games, and you know exactly squat about the Westchester Angel. Now you had better start talking as soon as I draw breath or we are out of here and you will not see us again. Start talking now."

"Okay! Okay! Okay . . . man! Heavy or what?"

I stood.

"I'm talking already! I was there! I saw the whole damn thing go down. I watched it! All right?"

I sat. "No. You're lying."

"I ain't lying! I was there, man."

"Prove it. I'm out of patience, Wayne. You need to keep me here and I am walking . . ."

"I was near the bushes, lyin' there just minding my own business, watchin' the stars, smokin' some weed, you know? And I hear this noise, like people strugglin', and I look over and I see this dude comin' down from the road, where there is a gate in the fence, and he has a chick with him and he is pushing her in front of him."

"Why didn't she scream?"

He started to laugh. "Well, I didn't ask her, Detective Stone Cold. I didn't think I was invited to that particular party. You feel me? But I *think*—and you know it was kind of hard to see in that light, at that time of night—I think she had a gag in her mouth."

"What time was this?"

"Now, let me see, you're gettin' very particular and maybe my memory needs refreshing . . ."

I stood. "You're full of shit, Wayne."

"Ten or ten thirty Saturday night! Man! Don't you *ever* let up? All I'm askin' for is a little two-way reciprocity, dude."

"Give me something I don't know, then we'll talk about reciprocity."

"I'm settin' the scene. Chill. So he takes her down, where it's kinda like a beach. You been there?"

I nodded.

"It kinda levels off toward the water, and there's grass and it's a bit soft there, so you can lay down. And he throws her down on her back, he pushes up her skirt, and he rides that baby. Man! And he's tellin' her to hold him. Weirdest fuckin' thing I ever saw. 'Cause she's got her hands tied, right? And he's kissin' her like crazy, and when he comes up for air he's sayin', like, 'Hold me, bitch! Hold me!' And she can't say nothin' back because he's in this kind of frenzy, kissin' her and stranglin' her at the same time. When he's done, he pulls up his pants, and he starts to drag her toward the water. I guess he's figurin' on dumpin' her in the river. But just at that very moment . . ." He leaned back in his chair and started to wheeze with laughter. "You would not believe it, man! I mean, what are the chances, right? That is the very moment a Harbor Patrol boat chooses to just cruise on by. You should have seen that guy hightail it out of there. Man . . . he was like a dog with a jalapeno pepper up his ass!"

I thought about it for a moment. "Did you get a good look at him?"

He made an exaggerated grimace, sucked his teeth, and drew a deep breath. "Well now, Detective Stone Cold, here's how I figure it. I have given you enough that you *know* I was there. And you *know* I saw what I saw. Now, I have smoked a lot of dope in my time, and I have snorted a lot of coke, and you know how it goes. That shit can affect a man's memory. Not so much that he forgets things for*ever*! You feel me? But just so much that he needs a bit of *stimulation* for his memory. Am I wrong?"

I sighed. "What do you want?"

He wheezed his unpleasant laugh again. "Man . . . *man*! I have spent my whole life askin' myself that, and I *still* don't know. What do you want, Wayne? The sweet lips of a beautiful woman, the taste of a *fine* cigar that has been rolled on the thigh of a *Cubana* . . ." He leaned forward across the table. "A cup of real coffee, man, so many things. Where do I begin to tell you, man, what I want when I have lost my freedom?"

I sighed, like I was really bored, put my hands on the table, and went to stand. "Well, Wayne, what can I tell you? If you won't tell me what you want, then we can't make a deal."

"Okay, okay, okay . . . You get me out of here, man. I can't be in here. This place is full of dudes who *need* to be in here. You know what I'm sayin'? Like, they *want* to be in here. It's like some weird shit, unconscious drive to be in prison and, like, *controlled*! But I ain't like that. I need to be outside. I am a free spirit. You get what I'm sayin' to you?"

I shook my head. "I can't get you out of jail, Wayne. You were found guilty of being in possession of cocaine. You have to do your time. It's the law."

"*You* can't get me out of jail, but you know a man who can. Am I wrong? You can make it happen, Detective Stone Cold. Don't tell me you can't, because I know you can."

I shook my head again and stood. "To do that I would need a lot more than a description of the crime scene, Wayne. You haven't told me anything I didn't already know . . ."

He smiled and interrupted me. "But I told you enough that *you* know I was there and I saw it go down. Think about it, Detective Stone Cold. Think about it and we are gonna talk again."

"Goodbye, Wayne."

"Goodbye, Detective Stone Cold." He leered at Dehan. "I'll catch *you* down the road, Detective Dehan."

Ten minutes later we climbed into my Jaguar—an original right-hand-drive, burgundy 1964 Mark II, with spoke wheels—and rolled down the windows to let in the sun. Dehan stared at me and I stared out the windshield.

She said, "I think he's full of crap."

I nodded several times, then turned the key in the ignition and fired up the big engine. As we pulled out and started the long drive across the dark water, I said, "I want to have a look at the place. I also want to have a look at what the press said about the murder, what details we released to them. We should talk to Ibanez too."

She raised her aviators up like a medieval visor and squinted at me, frowning. "He said something that caught your attention. He said something you want to check against what the press reported, because you think only somebody at the scene could have known it."

I laughed. "You asking or telling?"

"Both. I'm asking but I know I'm right. What was it? What did he say?"

"You remember I said something was curious, and you thought I meant the decay of the semen?"

"Uh-huh."

"I didn't. What struck me as curious was the fact that he had crushed her windpipe with his thumbs. But she was lying facedown."

She made a face and nodded. "So he was trying to move her."

"Right. The report you read made no mention of that. So I want to know if the papers or the TV did. Because if they didn't . . ."

She was nodding. "He did. He said the killer tried to move the body into the river, then ran when the Harbor Patrol came by."

"Yup. So we need to pull up the reporting from the time. Because if he was there, either he saw who did it, or . . ."

I looked at her and she said, "Or he did it."

TWO

We found a space to park outside the Golden Mango Supermarket on Havemeyer Avenue and walked the short distance to Zerega, which runs along beside the creek. There is a stretch between the quarry and the FedEx depot, about a hundred and forty yards or so, where the road borders the riverbank, separated only by an ugly fence made of steel tubing and wire mesh, about eight feet high. It serves little purpose, other than to make a place that should have been beautiful even uglier than it had already become: it was both easy to scale and easy to cut through.

Dehan touched my arm and pointed. "There's a gate over there. It's open."

I followed her over and examined the gate. There were scratches that suggested it had once been secured by a chain and a padlock, but both were long gone. Dehan pushed the gate farther open and we squeezed through into a miniature jungle of tall grasses, weeds, ferns, bushes, maples, and oak trees. I stood a moment, absorbing the scene. Dehan pushed farther in, following what might have once been a beaten path, taking big, arching steps over weeds and nettles with her long legs. She had the file with her.

I called out, "I think the body was down there." She turned to look at me and I pointed to the right. "There should be an inlet down there, with a rocky beach, and a grassy lip, like a small mound."

She nodded and started picking her way to the right a bit. I followed and we came out onto a sloping bank of mixed rocks, sand, and moss that descended steeply for about eight or nine feet to a small knoll, roughly oval, about twelve or fifteen feet long and six or seven feet across at its widest point. It was surrounded on three sides by tall grass and shrubs, but on the far side it sloped gradually down to a rocky inlet in the river. Dehan pulled out the pictures of the crime scene. "That's it, there," she said, and we scrambled down to the knoll.

She stood a moment examining the pictures again while I peered over her shoulder. She pointed ahead, to the edge of the grassy lip. "Her body was over there, facedown, with her right arm pinned underneath her and her left arm kind of flung out toward the river." She shook her head. "I can't make out any drag marks . . ."

I turned and looked back, in the opposite direction. "He probably rolled her. That's why her arm is pinned. If you drag a body you have to do it from the feet, otherwise they are almost impossible to move. If Wayne was telling the truth, he would have been over there, in those bushes."

I pointed up at a patch of undergrowth about thirty feet away. Dehan turned, looked where I was pointing, and nodded. She said, "So right now I am asking myself, if . . . *if* Wayne has knowledge of the crime scene and the position of the body, that was not made available to the media, what's to stop us from promoting him to prime suspect?"

I shrugged with my eyebrows. "I was wondering the same thing."

She echoed my eyebrow-shrug with her shoulders. "The only thing I can think of is that, if he was the killer, he would have to be really stupid, seriously stupid, to draw attention to the fact that he was here at the time of the murder. And he struck me as a lot of things, but stupid wasn't one of them."

I scratched my chin, still staring at the area where Wayne had said he'd been lying, getting stoned and looking at the night sky. He would have had a perfect view of the events. I sighed. "Agreed. He's not stupid, at least not in the sense of having a low IQ."

I clambered up to the spot, lay down, and looked up at the sky. I called down to her, "What did Ibanez make of it?"

Dehan was quiet for a bit, leafing through the file. "She didn't really come to any firm conclusions, but she speculated that the most likely explanation was that Angela, if that was her name, was a prostitute and was killed by her pimp or a client."

I winced, sat up, leaned my elbows on my knees, and stared down at her. "Did she offer any reason for that remarkable hypothesis?"

She kept reading and eventually said, "Well, if you can call it a reason, she says there doesn't seem to be any other explanation for why she would be at a place like this at that time on a Saturday night. She quotes some statistics: that a Hispanic girl murdered and raped in the Bronx in a lonely place of these characteristics is most likely to be a prostitute . . ."

She stopped reading and stared at me. She looked mad. I agreed. I felt mad too. "So basically she had no evidence and assumed because she was an Hispanic girl out late on a Saturday in the Bronx she was a whore."

"That's about the size of it."

I sighed and stood up. "This is not Hunts Point. It's one of the safest areas in the Bronx. Not just the Bronx, in New York. Whatever her statistics may say, the chances of finding a prostitute working this district are practically nonexistent."

"Plus, look at the way she was dressed. What was her line, Miss Demure? A flutter of the eyelashes is extra?"

I laughed. "Mmm . . . sounds appealing."

"Funny."

I joined her on the knoll. "Did they check NamUs?"

"There is no mention of that."

"Let's go talk to Detective Ibanez. I think this is a case of the same old same old, Dehan. A woman nobody cares about killed by a guy nobody cares about. You go through the motions, you don't get an immediate hit off the databases, so you file it under Don't Give a Damn and let it go cold." We started climbing back up the bank. I spoke over my shoulder as we climbed. "And let's look at women who were reported missing around that time. It will be tedious, but I reckon if we can get some idea of who she was, we'll get some idea why she died, and who killed her."

———

You could tell Detective Veronica Ibanez liked to think of herself as badass. She didn't wait for us to find her, she came looking for us. She was small, all her movements were quick, and she chewed gum like she was in a hurry to get it chewed. She shouted to me as we walked into the detectives' room. "Yo! Stone! You want to talk to me?"

She said it as she walked across the room with her chin stuck in the air.

I smiled and frowned at the same time. "How'd you know?"

She arrived at our desks as I was pulling off my jacket. She had her hands in her jeans pockets and was chewing furiously. "Inspector told me you was looking at the Westchester whore . . ." She grinned and made a small noise that wanted to be a laugh but never made it. "I figured you'd wanna talk to me, get my view."

"Yeah. Grab a chair."

"I prefer to stand. I get restless sitting down. Whatcha wanna know?"

Dehan sighed, dropped into her chair, and opened her laptop.

I rested my ass against the desk. "What made you think she was a prostitute?"

She shrugged. "What else? She wasn't doin' voluntary work out there at that time of the night, was she?"

"That was it?"

"What else?" she said again. It was obviously her go-to analysis. "If it walks like a duck and it quacks like a duck, it's a duck!"

I shrugged and gave a small laugh. "But she didn't look like a duck. Her clothes were sober, demure even. She looked the picture of respectable middle class."

She made a "pfff!" sound. "You ever worked vice? I tell you, Stone, you should take a sabbatical and work vice for a year. It'll open your eyes. You get whores of every color, shape, size, and persuasion! Ask Mo . . ." Mo was laughing like an egg custard. "Hey, Mo, you're writing a thesis on the whole gamut of whoredom, ain't ya? You know 'em all, huh? You dirty bastard!" There was a moment of generalized hilarity. She turned back to me. "Believe me, pal. Clothes don't mean nothin'!"

I was about to ask her how, then, she knew what a duck looked like, but I could see the discussion turning circular, so I left it and moved on.

"I saw in the file you ran her prints and her DNA, but there's no mention of NamUs. Did you check on women reported missing . . . ?"

Before I could finish the question she gave a big shout of laughter. "Are you kidding me? Do you know how many files on missing women there are? One hundred thousand, my friend! *One hundred thousand!*" She did a weird thing with her neck, moving her head from side to side. "If you think I'm gonna bust my ovaries goin' through a hundred thousand files looking for a babe who is probably an illegal *anyway*, so she ain't gonna *be* in those files, you are plumb crazy. No way. You wanna do that, be my guest. I got more important things to do!"

I heard Dehan's voice from behind me. "More important than identifying a murdered girl?"

Before she could answer, I said, "What steps *did* you take to identify her, Veronica?"

"You know what we did. It's in the report. We ran her

through CODIS and IAFIS, and we spent a day canvassing the area. Nobody knew her, nobody had seen her."

I heard Dehan snort. "A whole day, huh? You sure earned your pay that week, Ibanez."

I glanced around at her and smiled. She was staring at her laptop. Ibanez looked at me. "You know what, Stone? I don't need this."

I nodded. "I know, you have important stuff to do."

"Take a hike. You got any questions, look in the report."

She went striding at speed back across the room, with her chin in the air. I turned back to Dehan. "What are you doing?"

"I'm checking the reports from the time to see if there is any mention of the position of the body."

"And?"

"So far I've read three reports. None of them says anything about the position of the victim." She sat back in her chair and linked her fingers behind her head. "Seems to me that, if the media had been told that it looked as though the body was going to be dumped into the water, they would have reported it." She shrugged. "You know, bodies floating down the river, that kind of stuff. Sort of thing the press like."

"I'm inclined to agree. But keep looking. I'm going to look for women reported missing May and June of 2016. Veronica is probably right. It probably runs into thousands. But first, let's go and report to *El Jefe*."

We climbed the stairs to the inspector's office, tapped, and were told to come in. He was standing at the window, spraying something onto his potted plants. He smiled benignly at us and gestured toward his chairs. "Sit, sit. I am just tending to my plants. All life is sacred, don't you think?"

Dehan said nothing so I spoke for both of us. "Can't argue with that, sir."

"No," he said, lowering himself into his chair with a sigh. "And if you did, you'd be wrong. So, how did you get on at Rikers? Has he got information of value? Or is he bluffing?"

Dehan answered. "It may be both, sir. He has something, but it may not be as valuable as he is trying to make out."

He frowned. "I see . . ."

I said, "He claims he was at the scene."

"In what capacity?"

"Well, that's just the thing, sir. He says he was enjoying a joint, lying on the grass looking at the stars, when he saw the killer arrive with the victim. He claims she was bound and gagged. He described the way her wrists were bound and, more important than that, he said that after the victim was killed, the killer tried to drag her to the river. That is a fact that, as far as we know, was never reported to the media."

He nodded. "Aha, so if he knows that, either he was there as a witness . . ."

"Or he did it."

"Indeed. So what are your next steps?"

I drew breath but Dehan spoke first. "We spoke to Detective Ibanez. She couldn't add anything to what was in the report. So we thought we would check how the murder was reported at the time and see if there is any reference to the body's being moved. If there isn't, then A, Wayne becomes our prime suspect, and B, the chances are good he has more information to give us. Also, we start trawling reports of missing women around May and June 2016."

He frowned. "That wasn't done in the original investigation?"

I shook my head once. "Nope."

He raised an eyebrow. "I see. May I suggest you also approach the PDs and sheriff's departments of New Jersey, Maryland, Pennsylvania, Connecticut, et cetera . . ."

I nodded. "All our immediate neighbors. Yes, we'll do that. How we proceed thereafter, sir, depends very much on what we find regarding how the media reported the case."

He leaned back in his chair. "That makes perfect sense, Detectives. Well done. I won't hold you up any longer. Good work."

As we left he was reaching for the internal phone. As I closed the door we heard him saying, "Ah, Detective Ibanez, could you come up and see me for a moment . . ."

We passed her on her way up. She and I made a point of ignoring each other, but Dehan said, "Going to see the Inspector, Ibanez? Say hi from me."

She didn't answer.

We worked through lunch; Dehan read every article she could find on the case and contacted the major TV news networks for any footage they had where the murder was reported. Meanwhile, I sent out a request to the neighboring PDs and sheriff's departments for missing persons reports on Hispanic females in their early to midtwenties, reported missing in late May or June 2016.

After that it was a matter of trawling, painstakingly, through the NamUs database. Ibanez had not exaggerated. There were approximately one hundred thousand cases of missing women over the age of twenty-one, and an extra two thousand three hundred people reported missing every day. My search criteria were pretty narrow, but even so there were thousands of files to work through.

By eight o'clock that evening I was beat. I rubbed my eyes, crunched my vertebrae, and looked at Dehan, who was leaning back with a pencil in her mouth, reading from the screen of her laptop.

I shrugged and shook my head. "I haven't found her. I need food and a bottle of wine."

She nodded for a while, still reading. Then she yawned and stretched, reached forward, and switched off the computer. "Me too." She rubbed her face with her hands and stared at me. "It was not reported, Stone. However Wayne Harris came by that information, it was not through the press." We stared at each other for a long moment, then she summed it up. "Either he has spoken to somebody who was there and told him what happened, or . . ."

She shrugged and I nodded.

"He was there."

THREE

BY THE TIME WE GOT HOME IT WAS ALMOST NINE o'clock. Dehan put a couple of pizzas in the oven while I pulled a cork from a bottle of wine, then fixed a couple of martinis, extra dry, while the wine breathed. As I placed her drink on the bar, Dehan said, "So, Sensei, how do you want to play it?"

I thought about it. "First drink, then dinner, then bed."

"Where's your red nose, Mr. Clown?"

I carried my drink to the sofa, kicked off my shoes, stretched out, and spoke to the ceiling. "I say we don't rush our fences. Wayne ain't going anywhere anytime soon." Dehan came over, nudged my feet aside with her ass, and sat on the arm of the sofa. I looked at her. "He's playing it like he has a strong hand. Maybe he has, but we can bluff. I don't want to give him a deal if I can avoid it."

She nodded. "So, before we go back to him we try to find out who she is. Then take it from there."

I nodded. "I think that makes sense."

There was a ping from my phone. She retrieved it from my jacket pocket and handed it to me.

I thumbed the screen. "Emails," I said. "Whadd'ya know. Philadelphia PD and Boston PD." I pulled myself into a sitting position and read: "Reported missing June first, 2016, Sonia Ibarri of Buttonwood Avenue, Maple Shade Township in Philly. Twenty-two at the time of her disappearance."

Her eyebrows rose up. "Sounds promising, if that's the right word."

"Hmmm . . . We'll find out tomorrow." I went to the next email. "Boston PD. Rosario Clemente, twenty-three at the time of her disappearance. Reported missing Sunday the twenty-second of May, 2016. One week after our victim was killed. Also a good candidate. Neither of them is called Angela."

Dehan shrugged. "It could have been her grandmother's cross. Could be a family heirloom. They both sound like they could be our girl."

"We'll go see them tomorrow, have a look at some pictures, and hope we don't have to show them any of Angela."

She nodded gravely, then gently punched my knee. "C'mon, big guy. Pizza's ready."

———

Next morning Dehan phoned ahead to Alicia Clemente, Rosario's mother, and the Ibarris while I made breakfast, and by nine we were on the road to Boston. It was a three-hour drive, but we didn't talk much. We were in a somber mood. One hour in, Dehan, looking out at the woodlands and fields around New Haven, said, "It's hard to know what to hope for. You hope for a positive ID to be able to lay her soul to rest, and give some closure to the family. But you hope for a negative too, so you can give them some hope." She turned to look at me, with her aviators hiding her eyes. "We want truth and we want hope. It's a tough break when the truth robs you of hope."

There was no answer to that, so we drove on in silence.

At twelve we pulled into Dedham, in Norfolk County, on the southwest border of Boston. Their house was a large, attractive clapboard affair on Crowley Avenue, and backed onto a magnificent old Catholic church. I couldn't help wondering who on the town council had named the streets. Probably the same person who called the town "Dead Ham."

I followed Dehan up the stone steps to the porch and she rang on the bell. It was opened almost immediately by an attractive woman in her late forties or early fifties. She had made no effort to conceal the gray streaks in her black hair, which she had cut short. She was dressed in black Levi's and a denim shirt, and had a single string of pearls around her neck, which she fingered as she looked at us without speaking.

I said, "Mrs. Clemente?"

"Yes. Are you the detectives from New York?"

I nodded and showed her my badge. "I am Detective John Stone. This is my partner, Detective Carmen Dehan. May we come in?"

"Of course." She stepped back, holding the door. "Do you know something about Rosario?"

There was a hint of Latino in her accent, but it was more generic, cultured East Coast. Dehan said, "We don't know yet, Mrs. Clemente. That's what we hope you will help us find out."

She led us through a hall to a large, comfortable living room with dark wood floors, and two open sash windows set into a bow, overlooking Crowley Avenue. There were bookcases floor to ceiling in the alcoves on either side of an iron fireplace, and the occasional tables that flanked the old leather chairs and sofas all held large, interesting lamps—and more books: some open, all with bookmarkers in them. I noticed a couple were on architecture.

To the left of the door the room opened out to a set of French doors that gave onto a broad lawn. At the end of the lawn I could see the church. In front of the French doors there was a baby grand piano, and on it a photograph. I wondered if it was Rosario. Mrs. Clemente was gesturing us to sit, and saying, "Will you have some coffee?"

I shook my head as I sat on the sofa. "No, thank you. We

won't keep you long." She sat in the chair next to me, staring intently at my face. I said, "I realize you must have been through all this before, but it would be very helpful if you could tell us about Rosario, and the last time you saw her."

She sank back in the chair, her eyes abstracted. Outside the sun was bright and I could hear busy birdsong, but inside it was shaded and still.

She took a deep breath. "I raised Rosario alone. I was young when I had her. She was . . ." She made an expressive face. "A *mistake*! But she was the best mistake I ever made!" She laughed. "Bobby—that's her father—he was hot, you know?" She smiled at Dehan. "But I didn't want to *marry* him! Hell! I didn't want to have kids with him! We were at college, he was planning a career and so was I. But God decided he wanted me to have Rosario, so he busted the rubber and next thing I know I'm pregnant."

Her laughter was infectious. She flapped a hand at me. "You have to forgive me. I talk plain. I always have. It's got me into trouble sometimes, but hey! That's me. Anyway, Bobby panicked and ran, but my parents were fantastic and they helped me. Rosario grew up in a real close, loving family and . . ."

She paused, and suddenly her eyes were flooded with tears. She bit her lip and stared at me, with her head on one side, like she was begging me not to give her the news she feared I had brought.

Dehan said, "You had a good relationship with her."

She nodded, took another deep breath to steady herself. "Very good. People joked we were more like sisters than mother and daughter." She smiled and shook her head. "But it's not true. I was her mamma. And she is my little girl."

I leaned forward with my elbows on my knees. "Can you tell me about the last time you saw her?"

She gazed over at the open window with the fingers of her right hand resting on her pearls. "She had only recently graduated. She was clever, a real good student." She glanced at Dehan, like she felt they would share some kind of understanding about that. "She did architecture, like me. But she was interested in green, sustainable bio-architecture. It's a whole new field." She laughed again. "When I was a student we built things! Now they integrate materials!" She nodded, as though agreeing with some internal dialogue she had going on. "She was good, real good. So she got some interviews in New York . . ."

She shifted in her chair and frowned at me. "She applied only to small firms that were specializing in sustainable, eco-architecture. She didn't care about money. What she wanted to do was develop skills she could take to the Third World, because she believed a new model of sustainable economy would be born out there, like she said, from the roots up."

She took a big breath.

Dehan said, "She was an idealist."

Mrs. Clemente put a lopsided smile on her face and nodded. "She said she was a practical idealist. However, life teaches us there is no such thing. She was naïve." She shrugged. "But thank God for naïve people, right? Because they are the ones who do worthwhile things in this world. Pragmatists maintain the status quo. Dreams shake things up."

I gave a small laugh. "Maybe you have something there, Mrs. Clemente. She got some interviews in New York?"

"Yeah." She reached out and touched my foot. "I'm sorry. It's so nice to talk about her. All my friends are terrified of talking about her in case I cry. But it's a . . ." She shook her head and leaned forward toward Dehan. "It's a *fucking relief*!" She threw her head back and laughed. "Excuse me, but it is such a *fucking* relief to talk about her and laugh about her and *cry about her*! Why not? God gave us tears for a reason, right? So . . . !" She made an eloquent gesture with her hands, like things were flying around her head. "I am all over the place today, thinking about her. You asked . . . ?"

"Her interviews."

"Right. She had two. One was a smart outfit on Riverside Drive, on the Upper West Side in Manhattan. She wasn't so keen on that one. She thought the 'green' aspect with them was more for show. Then there was another one in Brooklyn that she was more hopeful about."

Dehan pulled a pen and notepad from her pocket. "Can you give us their addresses?" She wrote them down, then asked, "And were these both on the same day?"

"No, she wanted to spend a couple of days in New York. So she stayed with a friend."

Dehan stared at her a moment, waiting.

"Oh, um, Pam, Pam lived with her parents, Jason and Stella, give me a second and I'll remember. Hermany Avenue, twenty-two twenty, in the Bronx . . ."

I nodded and smiled. "I know it. It's not far from our precinct."

The words hung in the air like a bad omen. Outside the birds were still singing and the sun was still shining, but inside Mrs. Clemente had gone very still and very quiet, staring at me, taking in the significance of my words. Dehan was staring at me too.

I looked at her. "It runs into Zerega Avenue. Two hundred and twenty-two, would be about half a mile from the FedEx depot."

Mrs. Clemente asked in a dead voice, "What does that mean?"

I took a deep breath. "I'm not sure yet, Mrs. Clemente. Is that a photo of Rosario on the piano?"

She nodded. "Yes."

"May I have a look at it?"

She stood and walked quickly to the baby grand, picked up the picture in both hands, and brought it back, clasped to her bosom. Dehan got up and sat next to me on the sofa. Mrs. Clemente sat on the other side and handed me the picture. We all three stared at it together. The girl in it was beautiful. It was a graduation photo. She had her cap and gown on, and she was smiling into the camera. Her hair was black and her eyes were large, dark and humorous, like her mother's. She was full of life and enthusiasm, and dreams and hopes, but she wasn't Angel.

"This is not the girl we've found, Mrs. Clemente."

"Not . . . ? But the girl you found, is she alive . . . ?"

I shook my head. "No. The girl we found was murdered, two years ago."

"At the same time that Rosario was in New York?"

"About half a mile away from where she was staying."

"Oh, *Dios Santo* . . . !"

Dehan reached over and took her hand. "Mrs. Clemente, why was Rosario reported missing here instead of New York?"

"Because she left Pamela's house on Saturday morning, on her way home. Pamela left her at the bus station. She saw her get on the bus. Rosario was a very impulsive, spontaneous, independent girl. That's the way I brought her up. It's the way my parents brought me up too. I always thought maybe she got off somewhere on the way, to look at the sea or whatever. But she would have called, and by Saturday night I was worried. I called the cops, and by the time I filed the report it was, I guess, one o'clock on Sunday morning."

"So the report was filed here."

She nodded. "You think there may be a connection?"

I sighed. "It's impossible to say at this stage, Mrs. Clemente. Over fifty percent of the population of the Bronx is Hispanic, about half of them are women . . ." I shrugged. "What look to us like parallels may just be statistical facts. Let's not jump to conclusions just yet. We will look into this, we'll talk to Pamela, and if you'll give us permission to check her bank and phone records we'll try and build a picture of what happened on Friday and Saturday."

She nodded. "Of course." She fought to control the tears, frowning as though trying to make sense out of what was inherently absurd and cruel. "She is dead, isn't she?"

I held her eye and felt momentarily exhausted. "I wish I could answer that for you, Mrs. Clemente. I honestly don't know."

"The not knowing is almost worse . . . May God forgive me."

I nodded. "I know. We'll be in touch as soon as we have any

news. Is there somebody you can call on? Today is going to be tough. You'll be remembering . . ."

She echoed my nod. "You're kind. I have my work. Tonight I'll go and dine with my parents. We'll get through it together."

I smiled and patted her hand. "Sure. Feel free to call us anytime."

Dehan took a photograph of the picture with her phone and we stood. I hesitated a moment, then asked, "There is one thing, Mrs. Clemente. Have you anything—a lock of hair . . ."

She closed her eyes. "DNA . . ."

"Yes. Just . . ." I trailed off.

She turned and went to a dresser. There she opened a drawer and took out a small tin. She brought it over and handed it to me. "It's her first milk tooth. When you're done with it . . ."

"We'll bring it back to you."

Dehan gave her two kisses on the cheek and they hugged like they were family or old friends, then she showed us to the door and we made our way to the Jag, sitting old, sober, and burgundy in the May sunshine. I climbed in behind the wheel and watched Mrs. Clemente close the door. Dehan climbed in beside me.

"Is there any worthwhile profession," I asked the world at large, and Dehan in particular, "that does not involve dealing with human tragedy?"

"Lots, geology, physics, architecture . . . Stone?"

I turned to face her. "Yeah . . ."

"How much of your life have you not told me about?"

I grimaced and nodded a lot. "Why?"

"The way you talked to her. She said that the not knowing was worse than knowing . . ." She frowned and shook her head. "You said you knew. Sure, we're cops. All cops know that's true. But the way you said it, you *do* know. You know that from experience."

I shrugged. "One day, Dehan, but not today."

I turned the key and the big old engine growled. I spun the

wheel and we turned back, south, toward Philadelphia and the Ibarri family.

After about half an hour she reached over and squeezed my knee. It was a gesture that made me smile. I looked at her. She was smiling back at me, with the wind whipping her hair across her beautiful face. "You don't have to," she said. "You're an old, Anglo-Saxon dinosaur. I get that, and I like it. But when you're ready, I'm here."

I nodded. "I know."

And we drove on in comfortable silence.

FOUR

It was seven o'clock by the time we arrived at the Maple Shade Township and turned into Buttonwood Avenue. The Ibarri home was, like the Clemente home, a gabled, clapboard house. It was painted in white and gray, well kept and surrounded by well-tended gardens and lawns. It lacked the urbane elegance of the Clemente house; it had more the feel of a genteel country cottage. It was pretty and homey. Dehan spoke absently, half to herself: "I bet the kitchen smells of apple pie and baking bread."

I looked at her, nodded, sighed, and climbed out. The slam of the car doors echoed in the evening street and we followed the flagged path to the blue front door. It was opened by a man who looked to be in his late sixties. His black hair was receding and turning to gray, and he had a pair of gold-rimmed reading glasses hanging around his neck. Dehan said, "Mr. Ibarri?"

He nodded. "Yes, I am."

"We're Detectives Dehan and Stone, from the NYPD."

We showed him our badges and he nodded again and stood back. "My wife is in the living room."

The living room had the same cottagey look as the outside of the house. The sofa and chairs arranged around the coffee table were upholstered in white chintz with pink flowers that were echoed by the curtains. There were paintings on the walls of landscapes and kittens, and everywhere you could put a doily there was a doily. Mrs. Ibarri was standing in front of one of the armchairs, with her hands linked, one holding the other, in front of her belly. She was trying to smile, but her face was too rigid with anxiety. Dehan told her who we were and she nodded and glanced at the sofa and the chairs. We all sat. They didn't offer us coffee. Instead Mrs. Ibarri said, "Have you found Sonia?"

Dehan shook her head. "We don't know. We are hoping you can help us. When did you last see Sonia?"

Mr. Ibarri frowned. "We already explained to the police when we reported her missing . . ."

I said, "Was that the Philadelphia PD?"

"Of course."

"We are from New York, Mr. Ibarri. We only have the very basic information they emailed us. I know it is very hard to go over it again . . ."

He nodded. "No, I see." He stared down at the carpet. "Sonia went to New York on Tuesday, the twenty-fourth."

"May?"

"Yes, the twenty-fourth of May. She was going to stay there for a week, with Mary's sister . . ." He stared at us a moment, then gestured at his wife. "Mary is my wife. She is originally from New York. Her sister used to live there." He closed his eyes, frowned, and waved his hand at us, as though he was saying goodbye. "I am digressing. I mustn't do that. My father used to do the same thing. It's infuriating . . ."

His wife touched his knee. "Nelson . . . ? When we last saw Sonia."

He covered her hand with his and looked at her. It was a tender gesture, though he was frowning.

"She took the bus. She was looking for work. She was thinking of moving to New York. No disrespect." He smiled at us without much humor. "I can't imagine why, but she thought it would offer her more opportunities. Opportunities for what? That's what I asked her. 'Opportunities for life, Papito!'" He shrugged, then sighed. "Papito. That's what she called me. So she phoned us on the Thursday. We talked. She said maybe she had a job. She had met somebody who said he might have work for her. I asked her, what kind of work? She didn't go to college, you know? She said college wasn't for her. We told her, 'We'll pay, whatever it costs.' But, 'No, Papito, I want to work. I want to make money.' So she went to New York."

He went quiet, blinking, staring at the wall. Mary gave his hand a small squeeze. She said, "She told us Olga, that's my sister, Olga said she could stay with her as long as she liked. They were real close. Olga never had kids, you know? So our Sonia was like the apple of her eye. She loved her like her own child. When she went missing it killed her. Literally. She died like a month later."

Dehan had been making notes. Now she was frowning at her pad. "So she was due back Tuesday the thirty-first?"

Mary nodded. "In the morning. But Olga phoned me on Tuesday night. She was half crazy out of her mind, crying. She was hysterical."

"Why?"

They were both quiet for a long moment. Then he buried his face in his hands and started sobbing noisily. She looked away from him, then put her fingertips to her lips and blinked away her own tears. After a moment she said, "Sonia had met a man, a man who told her he could give her work. On Friday she told Olga she was going to spend the weekend with him. She was twenty-two, an adult, there was nothing Olga could do . . ."

Nelson's voice came shrill and twisted. "*She should have told us! An adult? She was a child! In her mind . . .*" He stabbed at his forehead with his finger, his eyes and his nose swollen with crying. "*In her mind she was still a child!*"

Mary sighed. "She begged Olga not to tell us. She didn't want to worry us. Monday she had heard nothing. She was sick, not knowing what to do. Tuesday she phoned me, crazy, out of her mind. So we called the police and we told them what had happened. They wrote it all down and we never heard nothing more."

Dehan took a deep breath and shook her head. "And your sister died, Mrs. Ibarri?"

"On the thirty-first of June. Exactly one month later. Her heart just broke, you know? She had the high blood pressure."

I knew it wasn't Angela, because Sonia was still at home with her parents when Angela was murdered, but I asked the question anyway, with a sinking feeling that I knew what the answer was going to be. "Where was your sister's house, Mrs. Ibarri?"

"In the Bronx, the nicer part. Virgil Place, in the Castle Hill area. Not by the PJs . . ."

I nodded. "I know it. Mrs. Ibarri, Mr. Ibarri, the girl we have found is not your daughter. The girl we found died before your daughter left home. But we are going to make inquiries and see if we can find out what happened to Sonia." I shrugged. "Sometimes people do crazy things, then they feel bad and they don't know how to make it right. So they don't call, time goes by, and every day it gets more difficult . . ."

She nodded. "Thank you. If you find her, tell her we're not mad. We just want to know she's okay."

"Of course." I paused a moment. "Mrs. Ibarri, may we have a photograph of Sonia?"

"Of course!"

She stood to go and get one.

I hesitated and added, "It's a long shot, but there is a DNA database . . ." They both stared at me. "It's for all sorts of people, not just criminals and deceased people." Even as I said it, I was aware how lame it sounded, but I pressed on. "Would you happen to have anything of Sonia's, a lock of hair, a hairbrush . . . ?"

Nelson nodded. He stood and went upstairs. Mary went to the fireplace and took a photograph from the mantelpiece. We both stood, and she gave the picture to Dehan. I looked over her shoulder. It showed two pretty girls on a beach, laughing and waving at the camera. They were similar, but one was slightly older. Mary said, "She's the younger one. The one on your right. She was visiting her sister in California. Her sister wants to be an actress, so she went to Los Angeles five years ago."

I studied her face and she looked away. "What's her name?"

"Annabel."

"You get to see her much?"

She made a face and shook her head. Dehan took a picture of the photo on her phone and handed it back. "We'll let you know as soon as we find out anything, Mrs. Ibarri."

Nelson came back down the stairs on slow, heavy feet. He was holding a hairbrush. I took it and examined it. It still had thick, black hairs caught in the bristles. I glanced at them both. "Has anybody else used this brush?"

"No, only Sonia. That was her brush. We've kept everything, just in case."

I pulled a plastic evidence bag from my pocket and slipped the brush into it. I looked at each of them in turn, wishing I could say something, give them some hope, but I couldn't.

"Thank you both for your help. We'll be in touch."

They saw us to the door, and we stepped out into the failing light of evening.

We had missed the rush-hour traffic, so it was a slightly less than two-hour drive back to Haight Avenue as dusk turned to evening, and evening closed in and became night. Once we were out of town, on the open road, Dehan said suddenly, "I heard what you said to Mrs. Clemente, there are so many Hispanics in the Bronx, the fact that her daughter and Angela happened to be within half a mile of each other may look to us like a coincidence, but it's not necessarily a coincidence." She shrugged, spread her hands. "It's like, how many white, Caucasian women were within half a mile of . . . I don't know, Sharon Tate, when she was murdered, right? I get it . . ." She sighed. "But I have to tell you . . ."

"Dehan."

"What?"

"I think we are looking at a serial killer."

She sighed again, deeper. "I knew you were going to say that. That's why you asked for the DNA."

I nodded. "We need to look for young women found downstream. We're going to find them." I shook my head. "No, that's wrong, we have almost certainly already found them. We just don't know it yet. We'll give Frank the samples tomorrow. We'll get a hit."

"Jesus . . ."

"It's days like this," I said, "I wish I'd become a geologist."

She stared at me in silence for a while and then started to laugh. "Isn't that what they call nominative determinism? A geologist called Stone! That would be something, wouldn't it!"

I looked at her and laughed. "I should have been called Ewan D. Pen."

She giggled like a child. "Or, I. B. Fuzz."

"Or, I. M. Porker."

She laughed out loud, and we continued in that vein for a good ten minutes, getting gradually sillier, until Dehan was curling up in her seat and wiping tears from her eyes. It wasn't that funny, but it was a release from the gloom of the day. After a bit we lapsed into silence again and the headlamps and the oncoming traffic outside the car acquired an almost hypnotic rhythm.

Suddenly she said, "What are we saying, that we have a weekend killer? Angela on Saturday the fourteenth, Rosario on the weekend of the twenty-first, and Sonia on the weekend of the twenty-eighth. That's a rampage, but only at the weekend."

I had been thinking the same. "It may give us a clue to his work. Maybe he worked nights during the week."

She was frowning at me. "Isn't that very rare in serial killers, to kill so close together?"

I shook my head. "Not really. There are no hard-and-fast rules about serial killers. There have been serial killers who have killed three or four times over several years, and then stopped, and there have been serial killers who have gone on sprees. You're right that the norm, especially when they begin, is to leave pretty long gaps between one killing and another. But then, typically, the gaps will grow shorter." I paused, thinking, and added, "We don't know whether he had killed before, and if he had, how many times."

She was silent again for a while. Then she said, "It may not be a serial killer, Stone. We are basing this assumption on some pretty thin evidence."

I smiled at her. "Like the infinite number of monkeys with typewriters?"

"Huh?"

"If you get enough monkeys with typewriters, one of them is bound to write the collected works of Shakespeare. If you get enough Hispanic girls in their early twenties in a single neighborhood, three of them are bound to disappear within a week of each other."

She sighed. "Okay, you made your point."

"If I'm right, his method of disposal was pushing them into the river. I'm not one hundred percent sure of the statistics, Dehan, but I do know that on average more than twenty bodies pop up each spring in New York rivers, as the water starts to warm. A lot of them never get identified, unless they have ID on them. He might have been killing for years."

"So his MO would be to pick up out-of-town girls, visitors, tourists . . ."

I nodded. "These three girls fit that pattern. They were also all three Hispanic, all three nice, middle-class Catholic girls, well brought up . . ."

"Yeah, they tend to fixate on a particular type of victim . . ."

"So, where would he pick them up? All three were in the neighborhood of Zerega . . ."

She interrupted me, "Don't forget, Sonia hooked up with this guy, was going to spend the weekend with him. That tells us something, right?"

"He's attractive."

"Right. He's attractive. He has some kind of magnetic attraction to a particular type of girl."

I nodded. "I got from Mary that maybe their two girls were a bit more wild than they liked to admit. Annabel went off to Hollywood, Sonia begged her aunt not to tell her parents she was hooking up with this guy . . ."

Dehan continued, "And Rosario was naïve, spontaneous, and independent. So we are looking at a guy who is attractive to a particular kind of girl: a girl from a nice, middle-class Catholic background who can, under the right conditions, be a bit reckless and daring . . ."

I took a deep breath, puffed my cheeks, and blew out. "And that's how he traps them. They walk away from him, they are safe. They go with him, he kills them."

"He could still be operating, Stone."

I grunted. After a moment, I said, "We need to go back to Wayne."

She was quiet for a bit. "You see Wayne in that role?"

I shrugged. "The problem with serial killers is they can be anybody. Yeah." I nodded. "I can see Wayne in that role, for sure I can. But I can also see Larry at the deli, Mo at our next desk, Alvin at the corner store."

"Mo is not magnetic or attractive."

"So Alvin is?"

"Well, you know, in a kind of nervous, spotty way."

"That's the last time you go to the corner store alone."

"Okay, joking aside, Stone. Do you think Wayne is the guy?"

I scratched my head. "Do you?"

She thought about it and finally shook her head. "No."

"Why?"

"Because this killer has been killing for at least two years, possibly much longer . . ."

I finished for her, "And the only reason we even know he

exists is because of Wayne. Why would he be stupid enough to draw attention to himself?"

"Exactly."

"Okay, but one thing we can be pretty sure of, Dehan, is that Wayne knows who it is. So we need to talk to him."

"Are we going to offer him a deal?"

"I'm not sure yet. He was very insistent that he did not belong in there, you remember? He's crazy to get out."

"Yeah."

"So let's see if we can tease something out of him with small offerings. Maybe we can draw him out with a visit to the crime scene, a coffee, small tastes of the outside." I glanced at her. "He likes to talk. He likes an audience."

"But if it comes to it, if he insists on a deal . . ."

I was quiet, looking at the long, dark road ahead. Finally I said, "Unfortunately that is up to the inspector and the DA. Let's see how it plays out."

And we drove on through the dark, toward home.

FIVE

"HER NAME IS ANDERSON? PAM ANDERSON? Seriously?"

She asked this the next morning, tying her hair behind her head in a knot to stop the breeze whipping it across her face. I glanced at her and saw myself duplicated, reflected in her sunglasses, looking back at myself out of a warped, bronze world as we sped toward the Bruckner Expressway.

"You are too young to know what that means," I said.

"Are you kidding? I was raised on repeats from the eighties. Pam Anderson. You think she has the . . . you know . . . ?" I glanced at her again. She was leering and nodding. ". . . You know . . ."

I shook my head. "You are a disturbing woman, Dehan."

"Pam Anderson . . . And she is coming to us?"

"On her way to work, yes."

"Will she come running, do you think? You know, down the street, boing, boing, boing . . ."

She started to laugh. I sighed and shook my head.

As it turned out there was little that was remarkable about Pam Anderson. She arrived at the 43rd punctually at nine and we took her up to interview room one. She declined coffee and sat across the table from us, looking vaguely worried.

"Pam, Detective Dehan and I run a cold-cases unit and, as part of a wider investigation, we are having another look at the disappearance of Rosario Clemente. We understand she was a close friend of yours and she had been staying with you just before she disappeared."

Her skin was pale, but her pink cheeks now turned a little pasty. "Yes, she attended a couple of interviews for jobs, one in Manhattan, the other was in Brooklyn. Our house was a convenient place to stay. Plus . . ." She sighed and looked down at the table. "We got on well and it was great to catch up."

Dehan was watching her carefully, chewing her lip. She asked, "So what day did Rosario arrive, Pam?"

"She arrived on the Wednesday, in the morning. Her interviews were on Thursday and Friday . . ." She trailed off.

"Did she meet anyone during that time? Did she go out, see anyone . . . ?"

Her eyes, very blue against her pale skin, darted from Dehan to me and back again. She shook her head. "No . . ."

I sighed. "What is it you are not telling us, Pam?"

"I don't know what you mean."

I smiled at her the way you'd expect a kindly uncle to smile right before he smacks you around the back of your head. "Here's the thing with cops, Pam: over a career as long as mine, you get literally thousands of people lying to you and trying to conceal the truth. You learn to recognize the signs pretty quickly, and here's the bit that is important for you: when you realize somebody is lying to you, that person immediately gets promoted to your suspects list." I leaned forward and put my elbows on the table. "Is that a place where you want to be?"

Her cheeks were glowing bright pink. "I don't know what you want me to say. She didn't . . ." She faltered.

"You were going to say she didn't go out, but she did, didn't she?"

"No . . . !" Again she faltered. "Not exactly. *We* went out, together."

Dehan shrugged. "Why is that a big deal?"

"It's not. You're making it into a big deal."

Dehan shook her head. "Come on, Pam. You deliberately concealed the fact. That means you didn't want us to know about it."

"What is it exactly," I said, "about going out with Rosario that you didn't want us to know?"

She buried her face in her hands and sighed loudly. Then she ran her fingers through her fine hair and flopped back in her chair. "Nothing," she said obstinately. "Rosario's mom, Alicia, is really cool. She is not a typical mom. She gave Rosario a lot of freedom . . ."

"But?"

"But it was freedom to *work*! Or improve herself. They got on real well, Rosario loved her and admired her, but there was always like this huge guilt trip. Even watching TV was like this big thing, you know? And when she came to see me I was like, come on! Relax! You will not go to hell just because you watch a bit of TV!"

Dehan nodded. "Or go out for a drink."

"Right! So we went out and had a few drinks. It wasn't like we got hammered and the cops had to take us home. We had a couple of glasses of wine and walked home."

I scratched my chin. "When was that?"

She looked at me with steady eyes.

I waited. "Pam? When was that?"

"Wednesday, Thursday, and Friday."

I smiled. "Every night."

"I figured she needed it. She was so uptight. And it was great to see her chill and relax. We had a laugh."

"You said you walked home. Where did you go?"

"Teddy's. It's like a ten, fifteen-minute walk from my house."

"On Zerega Avenue."

She nodded. Dehan was making notes. Now she looked up.

"I need you to think really carefully about this before you answer, Pam. Did anything happen on any of those nights, anything out of the ordinary, however trivial it may have seemed at the time?"

She looked around, as though seeking memories located in the various corners of the room. Finally she shook her head and said, "I honestly can't think of anything."

I gave a single nod. "But if you could, what would it be?"

Dehan looked at me like I was crazy, but the question didn't seem to faze Pam at all. She said, "Only that there was a guy who tried to hit on her. But that wasn't anything out of the ordinary. Guys were always trying to hit on her. She was beautiful. We ignored him and he went away."

I said, "That was Thursday, right?"

Now she looked a little surprised. "Yeah, Thursday."

"Tell me about Saturday morning. You went with Rosario to the bus station."

She looked over to her right, at Dehan's hands resting on her notepad. She shook her head. "There's nothing to tell. I drove her to the bus station. We had a coffee. She got on the bus and I came home."

I leaned back in my chair and scratched my head. "So, wherever Rosario disappeared, it had to be between the bus station and Dedham."

She shrugged. "I guess so."

"What did the guy look like?"

She frowned. "What guy?"

"The guy who hit on her at Teddy's on Thursday night."

She looked up into the corner of the room behind me, like there was a picture of him pinned to the wall up there. She bit her lip and her eyes drifted down to the tabletop and wound up looking at Dehan's hands again. "He was just a guy. I hardly noticed him. It was like two years ago."

Dehan was frowning hard at her.

I arched my eyebrows. "It wasn't like two years ago. It was

exactly two years ago, and Pam, I have to tell you, I think you're lying. I think you remember very clearly what he looked like."

Her cheeks colored again. "I'm not lying. He was just a guy."

"Black or white?"

"White."

"Latino?"

"No, I don't think so."

I shrugged and spread my hands. "So not an olive complexion, fair hair, blue eyes . . ."

"I don't know . . . no, not olive, white. I don't know what color hair. Dark. I didn't notice his eyes."

"Fat."

"No, normal."

I smiled. "Four foot three."

She gave a nervous laugh. "No, normal, maybe six feet. We were drinking. I was trying to ignore him."

"Armani suit?"

She sighed. "No, um . . . probably jeans, a pale shirt?" She hesitated. "Uh, maybe he worked there. I'm really not sure. It was two years ago and I *was* trying to ignore him."

I smiled in a way you could describe as knowing. "But Rosario wasn't trying to ignore him, was she?"

"Rosario was just real polite. She kept answering his questions and then asking him to leave us alone. You can't do that. If you talk to them, they stay."

Dehan said, "So she got into conversation with him."

"Not exactly, but in the end I had to say to her, you know, like, either ignore him or I'm leaving. Then he stopped and left us alone."

I nodded my understanding. "Sure, that makes sense. Was that why you didn't go with her on Friday?"

Her eyes went wide and her mouth sagged. "What?"

"Friday night, she went alone to Teddy's. Did she ask you not to go, or did you just decide you didn't want to be the spare wheel?"

"How did you know that?"

"Would you just answer the question, please, Pam?"

She puffed out her cheeks and blew out, staring down at the table. Then she held up her hands. "Okay, you got me. Rosario wanted to do the whole Friday night thing, party, have a few tequilas. That's not my scene. I like to go out with friends, have a few drinks, a laugh, and go home. Rosario is either one extreme or the other. Work, work, work, like a good Catholic girl, or, if you give her an inch, she goes crazy. So I told her I wasn't going and frankly I think she was relieved."

I pinched the bridge of my nose and sighed. "So she went to Teddy's to party with this guy."

"Pretty much."

"Did she come back?"

She sat up straight, wide-eyed. "Yes! Of course!"

Dehan spoke to the pad as she was writing. "But you two were kind of tense, right?"

Pam shrugged and sighed. "She came back at two a.m., smelling of booze, giggling and making a noise, bumping into things . . . I guess it could have been funny, but it made me mad."

I knew where Dehan was going, because I was headed to the same place. I said, "So in the morning you were not on really good terms."

She shook her head.

"You dropped her at the bus station but you didn't have coffee and you didn't see her onto the bus."

She went very still. After a moment she said, "She told me she didn't want me to stay. I was already mad that she had wanted to hang out with that dork instead of with me, her friend, and when she said that, I just dumped her bag on the sidewalk, turned around, and went home."

We were quiet for a long moment. Finally I said, "When she disappeared, you felt guilty. You felt people would blame you for letting her go alone to the bar, and above all for not staying with her until she got on the bus. So you lied."

She took a handkerchief from her pocket, blew her nose, and dabbed her eyes. It was the only indication that she was crying. "I felt so ashamed. She was my best friend, and a fit of stupid jealousy . . . Who could have imagined that a small argument . . ." She trailed off, then looked at me. "How could I face her mother, look her in the eye?"

Dehan laid down her pen and clasped her hands in front of her, as though she were praying. "Pam, do you appreciate how important this is?"

Pam frowned. "What do you mean?"

"Has it occurred to you that Rosario, after meeting this guy at the bar, arranged to meet him again the next day? That she didn't want you to stay at the bus station because she was not going to get on the bus, she was going to go and spend the day with the guy from the bar?"

Pam's pale skin turned even whiter. Her eyes stared and flooded with tears. She shook her head. "No. No, she wouldn't do something like that. No, you're wrong . . ."

I sighed. "Pam, it's not your fault. Nobody could possibly hold you responsible. She was an adult and she knew what she was doing. You were her friend, not her nanny. But we have reason to believe that this man may well be responsible for the deaths of three women. So it is really important that you try to remember everything you can about him; anything, the tiniest detail could prove crucial."

She covered her mouth with her hand. Her voice came muffled, "Oh God, Rosario . . ." and she began to cry. It wasn't now the restrained tears she had shown before, but the full, grotesque realization of what had happened to her friend. Dehan took her hand and held it in both of hers.

"He's right, Pam. Grieve for your friend, but you cannot blame yourself. If somebody hurt her, then the person who is responsible is the guy who did it. Help us to find him. Try to remember."

But she wept disconsolately for a full two minutes, and every time she tried to talk she dissolved in tears again. Eventually we had a car drive her home and she promised, among sobs, that she would think about it and see if anything came back to her. I didn't hold out much hope.

Downstairs I dropped into my chair and sat staring at the ceiling. Dehan rested her ass against the desk and looked down at me, chewing her lip. She said, "How did you know Rosario went to the bar alone on Friday?"

"I didn't, but it seemed a likely possibility. Pam was cramping her style and she wanted to know this guy." I shrugged. "And let's face it, somehow she wound up alone with the killer."

She tilted her head and made a face. "Good call." Then she added, "It's ten."

I nodded. "We'll go and see Frank, give him the tooth and the hair."

"What do you think?"

I rubbed my face with my hands. "If it's him, if he's our guy, our magnetic, charismatic Don Juan didn't make much of an impact on Pam."

"She described him as average: just a guy."

I sighed. "Caucasian, average height, nondescript dark hair, jeans or similar, perhaps a pale shirt." I snapped my fingers. "I just *know* I have seen that guy, somewhere. It was either in the States or in Europe."

"Could it be Wayne? Caucasian." She gave her head a shake. "Dark hair . . ."

"Wayne Harris is anything but nondescript. He's six four if he's an inch. He's built like a barn door and he has presence. You know he's there."

She nodded. "That's true enough."

I frowned at her. "Is he attractive?"

She looked surprised, then raised an eyebrow at me. "You getting jealous in your old age, Stone?"

"No, I'm serious. Is he an attractive man? We are speculating that our guy has a kind of magnetic charisma, right?" I shrugged. "You're a woman. Has Wayne got that kind of magnetism?"

She thought about it as though I had asked her to contemplate vivisection. After a moment she shook her head. "You're asking the wrong person. I detest guys like Wayne. He reminds me of Mick Harragan[1]. But I guess some women find that kind of dangerous, uncompromising guy exciting. He might lead them to take a risk, yeah." She shook her head again. "But, Stone, much as I would love to pin this on Wayne, like you said yourself, he is hard to ignore, he is not nondescript, he has fair hair, and once again, why would he implicate himself by putting himself at the scene?"

I nodded, sighed, and shrugged. She was right, and I had no answer to her questions.

She smiled without humor. "C'mon, Sensei, let's go talk to Frank. Then we can swing by Teddy's, *then* my internal clock tells me it will be time for a burger and a beer—and a think."

I stood and grabbed my jacket. "Ritoo Glasshopper, you are growing wise beyond your years."

And we made our way out into the bright morning.

---

1. See *An Ace and a Pair.*

SIX

"MY HANDS ARE FULL WITH THE RECENTLY DEAD."

Frank made this statement without looking up as he lifted the liver out of a cadaver that lay folded open like a book, from sternum to groin.

"Literally, not figuratively," I said, frowning from the doorway into his chamber of horrors.

"What do you want, John?"

"Just for you to notice me once in a while, Frank. Is that too much to ask?"

He nodded, squinting at the scales, and made a note. "What does he want, Carmen? Please make him go away. I am overworked."

"DNA."

"Oh, God."

"It gets worse," I said, pulled one of the chairs from the bench and sat. "I think we have a serial killer. If we are right, his MO means he could have been operating for years without anybody noticing, and he could still be at large. It's urgent. Very urgent."

He stared at me for a moment, then went and pulled the lungs out of the cadaver and weighed them too. Dehan placed the hair-brush and the tin with the tooth in it on his bench. "We need the

DNA from these two samples, and then we need you to run them and see if they match any victims pulled from the river since May 2016."

He made a note of the weight of the lungs. "Is that all? You don't need the name and address of the second shooter on the grassy knoll?"

I shook my head. "Didn't you hear? That wasn't Kennedy in the car. It was his double. Kennedy was abducted by aliens from the twenty-third century."

He put the lungs and the liver back where they belonged and sighed heavily. "Do you know what my wife said to me last night when I got home? She said, 'Who the hell are you?' My kids had grown up and left home. I never knew."

He peeled off his gloves. I said, "He's preying on young women, Frank. He rapes them and strangles them, then dumps them in the river."

"Everyone who gets murdered gets murdered, John. It's always a bad thing. Where are the samples?" Dehan showed them to him. He nodded. "Okay, label them for me. I'll get to them just as soon as I can." We stared at him without moving. He stared back, first at me, then at Dehan. "I'll get to them just as soon as I can, *today*! I won't have lunch. Happy?"

I smiled. "You're a good man, Frank. You deserve a better wife. One that hasn't got Alzheimer's."

Dehan shook her head and bent to label the samples. "That is so inappropriate, Stone."

Frank ignored me. "Don't expect a report. I'll run the results on my own time and give you a call if I get a match from the Jane Does. The official report will follow."

"I appreciate it."

"Now beat it and let me get on with my work."

We left him weighing organs and strolled out to where the Jag was sitting in a pool of dappled shade beneath a cluster of trees. There, I sat on the hood and phoned Rikers to make an appointment to see Wayne again. We fixed it for two o'clock that afternoon and took a slow drive down toward Zerega Avenue.

Teddy's Late-Night Bar was on the corner of Zerega and Lafayette. It was a broad, one-story building with an open parking lot on the Lafayette side. The door was open, but the lights were off in the windows and the sign said closed, so I put the car in the lot and we climbed out and made our way around to the entrance. Dehan poked her head in the door while I had a look at the outside. It didn't look like a clip joint or a dive. It looked like a respectable establishment.

I heard Dehan shout, "Yo! You the owner?" I didn't hear the reply, but after a moment she pulled out her badge and said, "NYPD, Detective Dehan," and disappeared inside. I followed.

It was a big, broad space with giant TV screens on the wall at one end and comfortable chairs and alcoves at the other, with a big, square bar in the middle. Right now it was dark and quiet with just one guy polishing glasses behind the bar. He was young, in his early twenties, tanned and blond. He was either from California or Australia. When he smiled and spoke I knew he was Australian, because he made everything sound like a question.

"Hi, guys. Teddy's not here right now? We don't open for another four hours?"

I smiled back. "Detective Stone. How long have you been working here?"

"Oh, just like, six months."

"Anybody here who was around a couple of years ago?"

He nodded. "Well, Teddy, obviously. And I think Crista? She cooks? You'd really have to ask them."

Dehan said, "You open at two?"

"Yep."

"What time do you close?"

He glanced from Dehan to me and back again, opened his mouth, and just said, "Ahhh . . ."

"We're not vice. We're not interested in Teddy's license. We're homicide detectives."

"Homicide?"

"What time does he close?"

He shrugged. "Well, it depends on the night? Monday to Wednesday we might close at two, or thereabouts. Thursday is generally a bit later? But Friday and Saturday, between you, me, and the fence post, we sometimes don't close till like four or five. This isn't going to get me into trouble with Teddy, is it? I really need this job, guys."

I nodded. "Don't worry about it. You're fine."

We stepped back outside and I stood looking up and down the sidewalk. We were five hundred yards from where Angela had been raped and strangled. I had a man who claimed he could tell me who had done it, but I felt I was going in circles, beating my head against a brick wall with no openings in it, anywhere. I felt a small knot of frustration in my gut. Dehan came up beside me and put her hand on my shoulder. "What now?"

"He's playing us."

"Wayne?"

I nodded.

"Like rats in a maze, we go this way and that, but in the end we have to go the way he says."

"You're exaggerating."

"Am I?"

"Yes." She said it emphatically. "C'mon! We've seen him once! He told us nothing. How's that playing us?"

I nodded again, more, and more slowly. "And now we're going to see him again, and he'll tell us something: what he wants to tell us."

She slapped my shoulder. "Come on, big guy. We'll go, grab an early lunch, and talk to him. Between us we can outsmart this bozo."

———

THAT BOZO ENTERED the interrogation room looking very smug and pleased with himself. He sat and smiled at Dehan while they cuffed him to the table. I showed the guard the coffee I had brought for him and said, "Can you leave his left hand free?"

The guard shrugged. "Your call."

Wayne leered at Dehan and as the guards stepped out he said, "Couldn't keep away, huh?"

I pushed a large cappuccino across the table to him. "Start with your bullshit and Detective Dehan waits for me in the car." I leaned forward, still holding the paper cup. "You feel me, dude?"

He looked at me with dead eyes. I felt in that moment that I was seeing him for the first time. I knew he would kill me without hesitation and enjoy it. He leaned forward. "I feel you, dude." He picked up the coffee and sipped. He smiled. "Good coffee. A man needs his pleasures, am I right?"

"Okay, you got your coffee. The cigar and the fresh air will cost you more than just proving to me that you were there. For a start, how do I know you didn't kill Angela yourself? I have to tell you that right now you are our prime suspect."

He looked at Dehan and smiled. "Oh, c'mon, baby. Me? You should know I am a tender and thoughtful lover. I would never hurt a sweet young woman with big, black eyes."

Dehan got up and went to stand behind me again, leaning on the wall. Wayne sighed, closed his eyes, and flopped back in his chair.

I said, "I'm waiting."

He gestured at Dehan with his hand. "She didn't need to do that, man."

"Stay on task, Wayne, we are both getting bored. Just forget Detective Dehan. Who killed Angela?"

"Yeah, man, get right in there. Bam! Who killed the little Angel? Well, you know what? You are not being very nice to me, *you feel me, dude*? And that affects my neurons. I don't remember so good when people are not nice to me."

"What do you want?"

"I want that cute Detective Dehan to sit here and talk to me."

"No."

"Shit, man . . ."

"Is that it? Are we done?" I reached across the table and took his coffee. I stood and handed it to Dehan. "Detective, will you take this, please? Throw it in the trash and wait for me in the car. I shouldn't be more than a minute or two at the most."

The door clanged open. Dehan left and it closed behind her. I sat and looked Wayne in the eye. It was not a pleasant sight. There was real hatred there. I leaned toward him. "Get this clear in your head, Wayne: You have needs, *you feel me, dude*? You have *needs*. Me? I have a job. If Angela's killer is never caught, I will not lose one minute's sleep. You? You will still have to serve out your sentence, and believe me, it will go on your record that you were not cooperative with the police in this investigation. Now, if you have something more than ten minutes of bullshit to offer me, start talking. But if I have to listen to another five seconds of your crap, you will have squandered the one and only chance you will ever get of a deal. I suggest you think hard about what you say next before you open your mouth."

He took his time about answering. When he did, he took a deep breath and said, "I want a deal. I can give you who killed Angela, but in exchange I want my sentence reduced to time served. Angela's killer is a dangerous son of a bitch, man. I ain't kidding. Me? I snort coke, I walk the line, I play around a little, but I ain't dangerous the way this guy is dangerous. This guy is sick, man, really sick. You fee . . ." He sighed. "You know what I'm saying?"

"I speak English, Wayne. I know what you're saying. Now, if you want me to even start thinking about talking to the DA about a deal, you need to give me something I can take to the bank. I'm not going to turn up and say, 'Hay, Darcel, I have a real strong feeling that that son of a bitch Wayne Harris is telling me the truth. Why don't you offer him a deal?' Do you understand that, Wayne?"

He stared at the wall for a while. "Yeah, I understand that, Detective Stone." He sighed. "Okay, how about you take me for a ride to the creek, and I show you where that boy hid her purse. You get her ID, you know who she is, you can give her family some peace and closure, and that will be proof positive that I was there and saw what happened. Will that be enough for you to take to the DA?"

"You saw that? I thought you said he ran."

"He did. He ran. He ran and hid in the bushes. So did I, man. That coast guard boat never saw the body, but if he hadn't'a run and hid, it would have seen him. Maybe me too. But once it was gone he come back, he took her things, like her purse and shit, and hid them. And I can show you where."

I studied his face for a while and he studied me back. Finally I said, "You want to give me one good reason why I should not arrest you right now for the murder of Angela?"

He made a face like I'd asked him if he believed in fairies. "C'mon, man! That is the stupidest thing I ever heard in my life! I'm in for five years. I might be out in two or three. Why would I deliberately implicate myself in a murder that would put me away for the rest of my life? That is just plain stupid, man." He stared hard at me. "I will tell you who done it, but I need that deal, otherwise I will not tell you shit."

I thought about it for a moment. On the basis of what he had told me alone I could have the whole area searched and find her purse myself. But the moment he told me her purse and ID were there, what had become of supreme importance was what he had not told me: what he had kept back. And he knew that as well as I did. I was still the rat, and I was still in his damned maze.

I said, "I'll talk to my inspector. If he agrees, we'll come and get you tomorrow."

He smiled and narrowed his eyes at me. For a moment he looked like a large snake. "I know," he said. "I'll see you tomorrow, Detective Stone Cold. Say hi to Detective Dehan for me. She is one cute babe."

I stood and went to the door. It rolled open with a loud, metallic echo. His voice stopped me.

"Tell me something, Detective."

I turned and looked at him.

"You getting any of that? I figure she likes it rough. Am I right?"

I left.

I found Dehan sitting in the car with the doors opened, listening to English Tudor music. She turned it down as I got into the car and looked at me. She said, "What?"

"We talk to the inspector and arrange to take him to the crime scene tomorrow. He is going to show us where her purse and her ID are hidden. After that, if we are satisfied, he wants a guarantee from the DA that if he gives us the name of the killer, he will get his sentence reduced to the time he has already served." I drummed my fingers on the wheel. "Effectively he gets released in exchange for giving us the name of the killer."

"That's some deal, but it's a fair price to pay for getting a serial killer off the streets."

I looked at her for a while. "I just hope we aren't helping to put one back on the streets."

"You still think he might have done it?"

"It doesn't make any sense. I don't know what I think, Dehan. Let's see what the inspector says and talk to the DA." I fired up the engine and sat listening to it rumble for a moment. Finally I shrugged.

Before I could speak, Dehan said, "Let's see who he fingers, Stone. If it makes sense, it'll make sense. If he's playing us, it won't stand up. All we can do is play it by ear and see where it leads."

I nodded. "Yeah, I know. Trouble is, we're playing his tune, and that is what I don't like. I don't like his tune."

SEVEN

THE INSPECTOR SAT STARING AT ME WITH NO expression. Then he blinked and turned the same stare on Dehan. Eventually he said, "What I like about you two is that nothing is ever simple with you." He paused a moment to think about what he had just said. "Still, I suppose the Westchester Angel case was never going to be simple, was it?" He sighed, scratched his left eyebrow, and then straightened it. "Let me ask you this, I'm talking about your gut feeling . . ." He clenched his fist to express the idea of a gut feeling. "These other girls, Rosario and Sonia, are they . . . ? Is it . . . ?"

I nodded. "We'll know more when Frank gets back to us, sir, but right now my gut tells me it's the same case. The coincidence is too great. They all disappeared within a week of each other, and within a stone's throw of Teddy's Late-Night Bar, and where Angela's body was found."

He placed one hand on his desk and drummed his fingers. "And of course you have to go back to that bar and talk to the owner."

"Yes, sir."

He spread his hands, still staring at his desktop, as though he was having a private discussion with an invisible advisor who was sitting there. "We have no choice." He looked at me, then at Dehan. "We have no choice," he said again. "If you are right and this is the work of a serial killer, he may well still be at large. *He probably is!* His method of disposing of the bodies means he may have been active for years, and is probably still active. We cannot afford to take the risk merely to keep a cocaine user behind bars."

"That's about the size of it, sir."

He looked at Dehan. "Carmen?"

"I don't see we have any other choice, sir."

He stared at her for a moment. "Of course, as John said, he may well be the killer, himself, and then we would be releasing the killer instead of locking him up."

"We have to take care that doesn't happen, sir. I suggest we take it one step at a time. Let's see what he gives us tomorrow and then take it from there."

He nodded for a long moment and said, "That's right . . . yes . . ." Then he turned to me. "Good, John, I'll call Rikers and arrange it. You go and talk to this, um, Teddy. See what he can tell us."

"Yes, sir. Thank you."

We went down the stairs in a somber mood and stepped through the doors into a late afternoon that had dusk on its mind. It was a short drive, a mile and a half down Soundview and Lafayette, with the sun glaring off the blacktop and the warm breeze reaching in through the open windows and slapping us around the head. It should have been agreeable, but I couldn't shake the feeling that, folded in somehow, behind all that sunshine and brightness, there was a darkness: a darkness that was watching us and smiling an unpleasant smile.

Dehan looked at me suddenly through the big, reflective lenses of her shades. "I don't like this case," she said. "You ever get that?" I glanced at her but didn't say anything. "I mean, you never *like* a homicide, but most cases, you get a handle on them and you get a feel and . . ." She trailed off, shook her head, and looked out of the windshield. "I'm talking crap."

"No, you're not. I can't put my finger on it, but there is something . . . *wrong*. I don't like it."

She nodded, big slow nods. "Yup."

We pulled into the lot at the side of the bar and stepped inside. The Australian bartender was still behind the bar doing something at the cash register. There was only one table occupied, by a couple deep in conversation. The bartender saw us, gave a thumbs-up, and called into the back, "Yo! Teddy! Someone to see you, mate!"

Teddy emerged a moment later. He had gray hair that had once been blond, tied back in a ponytail, and a long, forked beard that looked like it once belonged to a Druid, and had seen a lot of use since then. He had friendly eyes and hands the size of boiled hams, which he offered us with a smile when we told him who we were.

He pointed at a table in a corner and said, "Let's sit. What does the NYPD want with me? Can I offer you anything?"

We told him he couldn't, we sat, and he sat with us.

"How can I help you?"

Dehan pulled out her phone and found the picture of Rosario. "Do you remember this girl? She would have come in here back in May 2016. Ring any bells?"

He stared at her for a long time, but there was no recognition in his face. Finally he shook his head and said, "No. I mean, you know, she's a pretty, young Latina. You'd notice her, right? But that said . . ." He shrugged and spread his hands. "I don't mean to be inappropriate, but there are so many pretty, young Latinas in this neighborhood . . ."

She took the phone, swiped the screen, and handed it back. "How about this one?"

He shook his head again. "I don't know. Maybe I've seen her, but if I have I don't recall. A lot of people come through my bar, they would have to be either regular or very remarkable. One thing I *can* tell you is they were not regulars here."

I nodded. "How about Pam? You know Pam? She's pretty but she's not Latina." I smiled and he looked a little uncomfortable. "She lives in the neighborhood."

He flapped his fingers at his hair. "Blond, midtwenties, blue eyes?"

"Yeah."

"Yeah, I know Pam . . ." His face changed and he frowned. "Wait a minute, let me see that first one again. Pam used to come in here sometimes with a cute friend . . ." Dehan swiped the screen and handed him back the phone. He looked at it, frowning. "Yeah, maybe, could be. Pam had a friend, used to visit her sometimes and they'd come in here for a drink. That could be her. Nice kid, bright. They both were. But that is going back a bit."

Dehan said, "Last time she was here was two years ago."

"Seriously?" He made a face. "I guess that's about right, yeah. The other girl, I don't know."

I rubbed my chin. I needed a shave and suddenly wanted to be home with this case behind me. I sighed. "Okay, this is a long shot, Ted, but I need you to try and remember. Third week of May, two years ago, Pam and Rosario . . ."

"Rosario! That was her name!" He leaned back, smiling, and slapped his forehead. "Rosario!"

I paused, then went on, "Yeah, Rosario. They came in here midweek. They'd have been sitting, having a drink, and some guy started trying to hit on Rosario. Ring any bells?"

He frowned. He looked unhappy. "I run a nice establishment. People come in here, they feel safe. This is a nice, safe neighborhood. Okay, we have the PJs down the road, but it's like a different world." He shook his head. "A woman, or a young lady, wants to come in here alone, read a book or shoot the breeze, nobody is going to give her trouble here. Anyone tries that, they get kicked out on their ass. Excuse my language." This last was directed at Dehan.

"Don't worry. I hear worse at the station house. So maybe it wasn't a problem? Maybe he was just talking to them? Perhaps Rosario was open to it . . . ?"

He spread his hands and shook his head. "I'm open every day. That's seven hundred and thirty nights since what you're asking me to remember. That scenario must have happened seven hundred times in those two years."

I sighed. "Sure. Okay, how about a guy who frequented your bar at that time. He would have been here most nights, maybe had a habit of talking to young women, particularly Hispanic girls, who were either alone or at least not with a man."

He started chewing his lip and raised a hand like he was telling me to wait and be quiet. He stared over at the bar, but not seeing it, trying to see or hear something in his memory. "There was a guy," he said. "What the hell was his name. Casual . . ."

Dehan frowned. "You mean he was a casual kind of guy?"

He shook his head, almost impatient. "No, no. He worked here, like Pete." He gestured at the Australian bartender. "Casual labor, he was from Arizona or New Mexico, or maybe it was Southern California. Hell, I can't remember. But he was always talking to the girls. He especially liked the Puerto Rican girls and the Mexicans and the *Cubanas*. We used to make fun of him, but he didn't like that."

She pulled out her pad and pen. "What was his name?"

"*Damned* if I can remember! Just give me a minute. It'll come to me. If it don't, I got to have it written down somewhere." He frowned suddenly. "But he was a nice kid. He was never offensive to nobody. He never upset the clients or he would have been out before he could say *Viva Mexico*!" He glanced at Dehan. "No offense."

She raised an eyebrow and made a face of confusion. "None taken, Ted. We are going to need his name, and any contact details you have for him."

"Also," I added, "the days he worked."

"Oh, I can tell you that. He worked Monday through Friday. I remember that because, though he was a nice kid, he wasn't what you might call energetic. He just about got by on Friday, but Saturday and Sunday are busy days for us, and he just couldn't keep up. So I used to give him Monday through Friday."

Dehan glanced at me and I nodded. "Okay, we are going to need his name and details. Can you get them for us now?"

He looked from me to Dehan and then back again as realization dawned. "Are those girls okay? I'm pretty sure I saw Pam only recently."

I drew breath to answer, but instead I said, "How about Angela?"

"Angela?"

"About the same time. Again, pretty, well educated, used to wear a very beautiful cross around her neck . . ."

He went pale. "You're talking about the Angel."

I nodded.

He pointed at Dehan's phone. "They were killed?"

"We don't know."

He looked a little sick. "I never thought . . . Nobody ever asked me. It never crossed my mind. You think Jimmy . . ." His face cleared. "That was his name! Jimmy! Give me a second and I'll tell you . . . Fillmore. Jimmy Fillmore." He stopped dead, confused by his own verbiage. "You think Jimmy could have done that?"

I shook my head. "We don't know."

"If he did, he was picking up the girls here . . ."

"We don't know, Ted."

"So the Angel, Angela, she would have been in here."

"It's possible. Can you give us whatever information you have on him?"

He was quiet for a long moment. "I'll have to look for it. That has really shaken me up." He paused, staring down at the floor. "I'll have to look for it," he said again. "Have you got a card? And email? I can scan what I have and send it to you. Won't be much. Tomorrow morning?"

I patted him on the shoulder. "That'll be fine. Thank you, Ted. If it can be sooner so much the better. You have been very helpful."

He remained seated and watched us stand. "He was a nice kid. I mean, I hardly remember him. He just wasn't the sort of person you noticed . . ."

I paused, hesitated. "Do you know Wayne Harris?"

He frowned, made a face, shook his head. "Wayne Harris? Not by name. What does he look like?"

"Big, built like a quarterback, six five, solid muscle, short fair hair, blue eyes. Kind of guy you'd notice."

He spread his hands, stood, and smiled. "Sorry I couldn't be more helpful, Detectives."

We stepped out onto the sidewalk and I paused, with my hands deep in my pockets, to watch the long procession of head-lamps moving steadily through the gathering evening. The cool air from the river touched my face, and through the trees I could see trails of yellow light warping and breaking on the black water of the river. I felt Dehan's arm slip through mine and squeeze.

"Enough for one day, Sensei. Let's go home. I'll make spaghetti."

I looked down at her face. She was smiling, but it was a sad smile. I was suddenly overwhelmed by an awareness of my own good fortune, and, for a moment, I was terrified at how much I had to lose: what Rosario Clemente's mother had lost, what Sonia Ibarri's parents had lost, what we must all lose sooner or later in this world. I squeezed her arm tight, not wanting her to let go, and smiled. "That sounds just about perfect."

She gave me a tug toward the parking lot. A small gust of wind pulled a strand of her dark hair across her face. She smiled, with no trace now of sadness. I held her back a moment. "Carmen?"

She looked surprised and stopped. "Yes?"

"Would you . . . ?"

I stopped, hesitated, unable to go on. She frowned. "What is it, Stone?"

I took a deep breath and blurted out, "Would you mind if we stop on the way and get some fresh Parmesan?"

She raised an eyebrow and laughed. "Of course not. Weirdo! Come on, let's go. This case has me exhausted."

I climbed in behind the wheel and she got in beside me. The doors closed and we sat for a moment in the warm cocoon of old leather and walnut. I put the key in the ignition and paused. "Jimmy Fillmore. The invisible man. Mr. Cellophane."

"It's not an unusual type among serial killers. Withdrawn, shy, quiet, concealing a deep, passive-aggressive rage at the fact that nobody ever notices them."

I nodded. "I guess." After a moment I asked, "How did Pam describe him?"

"Uh . . . six foot, dark hair, jeans, normal."

Those weren't the words I was thinking of, but I didn't say anything. I fired up the engine, pulled out of the lot, and headed toward Morris Park. All the way I was thinking about Jimmy Fillmore from Arizona, and the way Pam had described him. What had she said? "I didn't notice him . . . I was trying not to notice him." And Teddy had said, "He's just the kind of guy you don't notice . . ."

But Rosario had noticed him, and gone back to see him again on Friday night, and probably arranged to meet him Saturday morning. She had definitely noticed him.

I pulled up outside what I had come to think of as "our" house, killed the engine, and turned off the lights. I turned and smiled at Dehan. She was watching me carefully. I said, "What?"

She raised an eyebrow. "What happened to the fresh Parmesan?"

"Oh . . ."

"What were you going to ask me?"

I shook my head. "I have no idea what you mean, and also, I need a martini, *muy seco!*"

I opened the door. She said, "Stone!"

"*Muy seco,* Carmencita*! Ahora!*"

I climbed out; she climbed out after me and slammed the door. "You're a dork, Stone."

"Martini, Carmencita! *Ahora! Muy seco! Ándale! Ándale!*"

She made her way to the door, pulling the key from her pocket and shaking her head.

EIGHT

THE PHONE RANG AT FIVE THIRTY IN THE MORNING. Dehan covered her head with the pillow and I fumbled on the bedside table. I finally found it, pulled myself to a sitting position, and pressed green. Frank's voice said, "Did I wake you?"

I frowned as much as I was able and looked at my clock. "No," I said malevolently. "I was doing my tax returns."

"Good, because I haven't been to bed yet. My wife's attorney just left. He delivered the divorce papers."

"You're lying, Frank. How can she divorce you if she doesn't remember who you are?"

"You're funny, deep down funny . . ."

"Yeah, I know, where it's not like funny anymore. Why are you calling me at five thirty in the morning, Frank?"

"Because, you son of a bitch, you were right. I got a hit on each one of them. Sonia Ibarri and Rosario Clemente." He sighed like a man who finds life depressing and death poor consolation.

I sighed back at him and sat up a bit straighter. "Ah, *hell*! I had half hoped I was wrong, Frank."

"I know, John. So did I. They were found within a few days of each other, end of June 2016. From what I can tell the MO was pretty much the same. They had been in the water a long time, but the wrists were still tied with silk and there was a lot of bruising on the mouth and throat."

"Where were they found? Mouth of the creek?"

"Rosario was washed up on Ferry Point Park, Sonia had drifted right out to Kane's Park, Shorehaven. You have a serial killer, Stone. He could be out there killing still."

"I know. Thanks, Frank. I appreciate it."

"Good luck."

He hung up. I put the phone on the bedside table and sat with my elbows on my knees. I felt Dehan's hand on my back and turned to look. She was sitting up, watching me. "He found them," I said. "Ferry Point Park and Shorehaven. End of June, a month after they were killed."

She nodded once and spread her fingers on her lap. "We have to make that son of a bitch talk."

I sighed. "If he hadn't contacted us, we wouldn't even know this killer existed."

She was quiet for a moment. "You starting to think he's on the level?"

I slid down and lay back with my head on her lap, staring at the ceiling. "Right now, I have no idea what to think. None of it makes much sense, Carmen."

"Come on, big guy. We don't need to be up for another couple of hours. Get back into bed."

I did as I was told, but despite the promise in her voice she fell asleep on my shoulder within a couple of minutes, and I spent the next two hours staring at the ceiling and thinking. And that was when, slowly, things began to fall into place and make sense. Others made no sense at all.

Or at least, I thought they didn't.

———

WE COLLECTED Wayne at ten that morning. He was handed into our custody and we led him, manacled at his wrists and ankles, to the Jag. All the way he had a smug, complacent smile on his face. When he was settled in the back, he leered at me in the mirror and said, "Nice ride, Detective Stone Cold. Ain't Detective Dehan goin' to ride with me, in case I misbehave?" He shifted his eyes to the back of her head. "You wanna be with me if I misbehave, don't you, Detective Dehan?"

We pulled out of the lot and started the long drive across the dark water of the East River. He was chuckling to himself in the back. "I guess," he said, "this is like our first date, huh? Our first time goin' out together. I have this feelin' that you and me could have a real special kind of relationship, huh, Carmen?"

"You want to get an answer out of me, Wayne, you call me Detective. Now keep your mouth shut. I'm tired of listening to your bullshit."

His laugh was like a wheeze. "I do like a strong woman, don't you, Detective Stone? It must be satisfying living with a strong woman like Carmen. Am I right, Detective Stone Cold?"

I studied him in the mirror for a moment. "You been researching me, Wayne?"

"Well, you know what they say, Detective Stone: Know thine enemy."

"Am I your enemy, Wayne?"

Again the wheezing laugh. "Oh, you know it, Detective. You are the system, and the system is my enemy. Now, Carmen, well, Carmen is a whole different story. Underneath that hard, NYPD career woman exterior lies the wild, free spirit of a Native American, and a Jew. Baby, you must have a troubled soul, I tell you. I know just what that is like because I have a troubled soul too. And you and me, I just know we could get real close."

She glanced at me. I couldn't make out if she looked worried or mad. I said, "Shut up, Wayne."

"I get a lot of time to read, you know? An' I like to read. I have a very high IQ. Did you know that? One hundred and forty-five. That makes me officially a genius. You know what I like to read about?" We didn't answer but he told us anyway. "I like to read about psychology. And do you know where people bond? Do you know where the links are forged that bind people's souls together?"

We were crossing the Robert F. Kennedy Bridge onto Randalls Island. Dehan looked at me again. "Do we have to listen to this?"

He laughed again. "I am getting to you, sister. Don't deny it. Let me tell you, those links are forged in the deep darkness of the unconscious mind, where what they call the primal impulses are at work. You see a man like me, and you recognize a natural mate, and there ain't nothin' you can do about it. All the civilized conditioning just falls away, man, and you are exposed, naked in the darkness of your instincts."

I shook my head. "No," I said. "You don't have to listen to this, Detective. There is stuff you can be doing at the station. You can follow up on the interview we had last night . . ."

Wayne threw himself back in the seat and shouted. "Oh come on, man! Jesus! Lighten up, will ya! I'm just playin' around! I'm jokin', man!"

I snapped, "You see anyone laughing, Wayne?" I waited but he didn't answer. I went on. "Let me tell you something. I don't think you can focus on the job in hand when Detective Dehan is around. And I think there is a very particular reason for that. I'm developing a theory. I think you have an unhealthy obsession with Hispanic women. I think you have a tendency to develop unhealthy obsessions about particular Hispanic women. What do you think, Wayne? What would I find if I started to explore into your past? Would I find the cause for that obsession? How about it, Sigmund?"

He didn't answer. I watched him a moment in the mirror. His expression was sullen. I pressed him. "You've gone awful quiet, Wayne. What's the matter? You don't want to play around and joke anymore?"

We drove the rest of the way in silence and pulled up at the back of the Golden Mango, on Zerega Avenue, at just before eleven. We pulled him out of the car, walked him through the gate onto the scrubland, and Dehan removed the manacles from his ankles. When she stood, she leaned close into his face. "Don't make me shoot you, Wayne."

He smiled. "See? I knew you was one of mine."

I said, "Okay, we're on the clock. Where is this purse?"

He looked at me and there was real contempt in his face. "Give me a minute, dude. It's been a while. I need to get back to the place, remember it, feel it. Know what I'm sayin'?" He pointed with both hands to where Dehan and I had been previously. "It was down there."

I glanced at him. "You sure?"

"Yeah, I'm sure!"

Dehan went ahead of him and I stayed close behind. Pretty soon we had come to the mound where Angela's body had been found. He stood looking at it and smiling for a while. Then he turned and looked around behind him, searching. Finally he jerked his head toward the place where I had lain. "That's where I was, chillin', enjoyin' a smoke. You ever smoke a joint, Carmen?" He looked at me. "Hey! I'm just making conversation, man. That's where I was. I heard them comin' down where we just come. He threw her on the ground right here, went down on top of her, and . . ." He smiled at Dehan. "He just choked the life out of that little girl while he kissed her."

I said, "That's old news, Wayne."

He studied me with hooded eyes. "You a real pain in the ass, you know that, Detective Stone Cold?"

I stepped toward him and shoved him toward the path. "Come on! I've had as much of your bullshit as I can take. We're going back. Come on!" I shoved him again and he stumbled. "Back to the car. You don't know jack! You think you can play games with me? Get moving!" I shoved him a third time and he almost fell.

"*Wait a minute!*" His face was flushed.

I advanced on him and shoved him again. "Move!"

"It's over there, for cryin' out loud!"

I grabbed him by the scruff of the neck and pulled his face close to mine. "Right now the DA is in discussions about your deal, Wayne. If we walk back up that path and get into my car, it's over! We are done! And we don't come back! So cut the Hannibal Lecter act and get the damned purse! *Do you feel me, dude?*"

He took his time studying my face in careful detail. Then he pulled away from me and started to walk. It was about a hundred yards, maybe a little less, over loose rocks and puddles, and through coarse undergrowth and tall grass, to a steep bank overgrown with dense trees and bushes at the foot of the GVC depot. He stood staring at it for a long while. It was hard to read the expression on his face, until finally he smiled and started moving up, into the undergrowth. He dropped to his knees at the foot of a pin oak and started to dig. After a minute or so, he pulled out a small ladies' handbag. He turned awkwardly, holding it in both hands because of his cuffs, and showed it to Dehan.

I pulled an evidence bag from my pocket, took the bag from him, and slipped it in. I said, "Back up," and as he came down the slope I said to Dehan, "You want to take a look?"

She nodded, pulled on some surgical gloves, and scrounged around where Wayne had been digging. She turned to me and shook her head. "Nothing I can see, but we better get a team here anyway. Just in case."

She called for a CSI team as we made our way back toward the car. Wayne spoke as he stumbled behind her and in front of me. "Hey, I did my part, right? I have proved I was a witness here that night. Now you got to get me that deal, man."

Dehan looked back at me. "They're on their way."

I shoved Wayne in the back of the Jag, hunkered down by the open door, and looked into his eyes. They were half-closed, and I could see nothing but contempt in them. I said, "When the crime scene team arrive we'll take you back to the prison. Then we'll examine the evidence. If it's any good, then I'll recommend to my inspector that he recommend to the DA that they go ahead with a deal. Now, before I do any of that, Wayne, let me ask you something."

"Knock yourself out."

"Do you know who killed this girl?"

He nodded. "I will name him for you. And when you check it out you will see I ain't lyin'."

The CSI van arrived ten minutes later. We told them where the site was and took Wayne back to Rikers. All the way there he was quiet, but every time I looked at him in the mirror he was watching Dehan, staring at the back of her head.

We handed him over and drove slowly back to the station. At our desk Dehan pulled a chair next to mine and we sat and emptied the contents of the purse. There was an ID card, a driver's license, a set of keys, some eye shadow, an eye pencil, a cell phone, and a handkerchief.

The girl in the photographs on the driver's license and the ID card was Angela. There was no doubt about it. She had been very pretty, and the smile in the pictures looked easy and natural. Her name was Angela Fernandez, and she was from Berwick, in Pennsylvania. Somewhere in Berwick, Pennsylvania, at that moment, her parents were still waiting for her, hoping.

I said, "We need to show this to the inspector. It looks like Wayne will be getting his deal."

She studied my face a moment. "You're not happy about that, are you?"

I shook my head.

"That comment you made about his obsession with Latinas . . ."

"What about it?"

"Are you sure you're being objective?"

I raised an eyebrow. "Explain."

"He was coming on very strong to me. He was being pretty threatening. Maybe you feel I am at risk and that's clouding your judgment."

I shook my head.

She went on. "Stone, I agree with you, he is a lowlife and I don't want to see him walk. But he has no priors for rape, sexual assault, or violence. And"—she shrugged—"let's face it, other than the way he was coming on to me, and the fact that I happen to be half Mexican, you have no reason to believe he has an unhealthy obsession with Hispanic women."

I nodded. "I have."

"What?"

"The way he reacted when I said it. I was flying a kite, Dehan. I wanted to see his reaction. I touched a nerve. That man is dangerous, and I really don't want to see him walk."

She sighed. "Well, he's probably going to and there isn't much we can do about it. Either way, Stone. I think this is as much about your protective dinosaur instincts as it is about anything else. I don't like him, but I don't think he's as dangerous as you say he is. He's just a dopehead and a scumbag."

I stared down at the items on the desk in front of me. Then I looked her in the eye. "Just keep an open mind, Dehan, please? Until we have this wrapped up. There is more to this guy than meets the eye."

She frowned, but nodded. "Sure. No problem, Stone."

"Right." I took a deep breath. "Let's go talk to the inspector."

NINE

INSPECTOR JOHN NEWMAN LOOKED DEPRESSED. "POOR child . . ." He'd said it a couple of times, now he repeated it. "Poor child. You'll talk to the family?"

"Detective Dehan just called her mother, Elisa Fernandez. It's two and a half hours' drive. We'll break the news to her when we get there, then see if we can find out what Angela was doing here, who she was with . . ." I trailed off and spread my hands.

Dehan added, "And if she had any connection with Teddy's Late-Night Bar or James Fillmore."

The inspector frowned. "I have to say, it is one hell of a coincidence that three such similar girls should have been connected with that bar, all within a few days of each other."

I sucked my teeth. "We don't know they were, sir. Sonia Ibarri was staying with her aunt, less than ten minutes' walk away, but we don't know that she had any actual connection with the bar. At the moment all we can say is that the connection between the girls appears to be their proximity to the bar. We'll see if that holds true with Angela."

He grunted and nodded.

Dehan smiled. "Like Stone pointed out to me, sir, there must be an awful lot of good, Catholic, pretty Hispanic girls in that neighborhood. The coincidence is maybe more apparent than real."

He shrugged with his eyebrows instead of his shoulders. "I take your point."

I said, "However, I am inclined to believe that the killer has some connection with the bar, because that was where Rosario went on the Friday night and, presumably, made an appointment to meet her killer on Saturday."

He narrowed his eyes at me. "And that does rather point to James Fillmore being our man, doesn't it, John?"

I had to agree. "Yes, sir, it does."

"But?"

"But there is one man, and at the moment only one man, that we know for sure was at the scene of Angela's murder, and who knew exactly where her purse was hidden, and that is Wayne Harris."

He frowned. "It doesn't make a lot of sense that he should implicate himself unless he is pretty sure of his information."

Dehan looked at me. "You said it yourself, we wouldn't even know there was a serial killer if he hadn't contacted us."

"I know, but, sir, for the record, I believe we should pull him in and interrogate him, threaten to charge him with all the murders. If he knows who the killer is, he will tell us. If he doesn't, then we'll know it's him." I shrugged. "How did he know *exactly* where the purse was?"

He rubbed his chin and heaved a deep sigh. "I do take your point, Stone, don't think that I don't. I'll discuss it with the DA and I'll tell her how you feel. The crucial point here is that we have a serial killer on our hands who, as we have said before, may have been operating for a long time, and may still be active. That means he has to be stopped at all costs, as soon as is humanly possible." He gave me a look that was loaded with meaning. "Meanwhile, you'd better get on your way to see the Fernandez family. Do give them my deepest condolences. I'll have this stuff sent over to the lab, and I'll put in a request for Angela's bank and phone records."

We thanked him and stepped out into the bright sunshine. A small breeze was moving the broad leaves of the plane trees on Story Avenue. We climbed into the Jag in silence and I turned the key in the ignition. As I backed out of the lot, Dehan was watching me, with her glasses sitting on top of her head.

"What is it, Stone? I've never known you to get so personal about a case. What's eating you?"

I didn't answer until I was accelerating onto the Bronx River Parkway. Then I said, "I don't know exactly, Dehan. Small things."

"Like?"

"Okay, for starters, the place where Wayne says he was lying smoking his joint the night Angela was killed."

"What about it?"

"Did you try it out?"

"What, lie there? You know I didn't."

"I did. It was really uncomfortable. There were sharp rocks embedded in the earth, there were a million small, sharp stones, and there were prickly shrubs and nettles. There was no way he was lying there."

She made a face. "Okay, that's odd, but it was May, and warm, so maybe he was lying on his jacket."

"But why go there at all? The obvious place to lie, which has easy access, is the soft turf where Angela was killed. It is completely invisible from the road. That's why the killer chose that spot to kill her."

She sighed. "Okay, you have a point. It is odd, but it is not conclusive."

"Another thing. When we took Wayne to the scene, he didn't follow the track to where he said he'd been lying. He paused, got his bearings, and took us down the track to the spot where Angela was killed. Then, once there, he had to stop and look for the spot where he said he had been lying."

She made a face that was skeptical and asked, "Anything else?"

"Yeah. There was no way he saw the killer hide those things from where he claims he was lying. He needed to get right up close to find the spot. That means he originally memorized the spot from up close. That was the image—the memory—he had in his head."

She thought about that for a moment. "Maybe he went up after the killer had gone and found the spot." She shrugged. "Maybe he hid the stuff himself."

I gave a small laugh. "Or maybe he killed her."

"We've been over this, Stone. He has no record of violence. Okay, he looks pretty intimidating, but there isn't a single assault on his rap sheet. No rapes, no sexual assaults . . . nothing!"

"And you can be damn sure, Dehan, that the killer's rap sheet is the same." I looked at her. She was frowning and confused. I explained. "This killer is smart enough to have devised a way of raping and killing, and disposing of the bodies, that eliminates all forensic evidence, and any trace that there was a serial killer involved at all. His rap sheet is going to be like Wayne's: clean of any serious offenses."

She shook her head and looked away at the spring skyline slipping past. "Stone, just this once, I have to say I don't agree with you. You know I admire you as a detective, but this time I think you are letting your personal feelings get in the way."

I smiled. "My personal feelings? You mean the way he comes on to you?"

"That doesn't bother you?"

"Of course it does. And it bothers me how close you are to the model of his victim of choice. And it bothers me that you can't see that." I glanced at her. "But it doesn't bother me enough to cloud my judgment. We'll follow the evidence, Dehan. Wherever it may lead. And if I am wrong, so be it."

We didn't touch on the subject again, though it played on my mind all the way to Berwick, and by the time we had pulled into East 8th Street and parked outside Elisa Fernandez's house, I was still no clearer in my mind as to the explanation for Wayne's apparently paradoxical behavior.

From the front the house looked like a cute, clapboard cottage, with a veranda cluttered with potted flowers and plants, a white, wrought iron table, and a couple of rocking chairs. It was set in a broad expanse of lawn, with an uneven paved path that led through it to the house.

The door opened before we reached it and a woman who was no more than five foot two, with neat, permed silver hair and a face that was still pretty but must once have been beautiful, greeted us with large, smiling brown eyes.

I returned the smile. "Mrs. Fernandez?"

"That's me." She had no accent. "You the police from New York?"

We showed her our badges. She glanced at them and said, "Come on in. I made some lemonade for you, but you can have coffee if you'd rather."

Lemonade sounded good and we told her so. She had a living room cum diner that was spotlessly clean and neat. Every cushion and every ornament was positioned with precision, and there was not a trace of a crease or dust anywhere. She sat us at the dining table where, I guessed, she thought we'd cause the minimum of disruption to her order, and went to the kitchen. She came back with a large glass jug of lemonade on a tray and three glasses. When she had poured and mopped up the drips, she sat and looked at us. She had a smile fixed in place, but you could see the fear and apprehension in her eyes. It was the expression of a person who has become habituated to being hurt by life and is just waiting for the next blow to fall.

I took a deep breath and made eye contact. "Mrs. Fernandez, I'm afraid I have very bad news for you. We have found your daughter Angela, and she is dead."

She gave a small gasp and crossed herself. Her eyes went red and spilled tears. She took a handkerchief, dabbed her eyes, and blew her nose. "It's okay," she said. "She is with the Good Lord. I've known for a long time that He had taken her."

Dehan frowned. "How did you know that?"

She shrugged and smiled again, like the answer was obvious. "She would have called, or written. She was such a good girl. She was a saint. She was too good for this world. That is why the Lord took her. When a week went by, I knew it was serious. After two weeks, I knew something real bad had happened. After a month, I knew she was dead." She reached out and covered Dehan's hand with her own. "When you called, I knew you were coming to tell me you had found her. She is with God, and with the angels, my little Angel."

Suddenly she was sobbing violently, with her eyes closed and the handkerchief pressed over her mouth. She didn't say anything, just made wrenching, visceral noises while she sat, stiff and erect, weeping into her neatly folded handkerchief. Dehan pulled her chair over and sat with her arm around her shoulder, not saying anything, just holding her gently. I wondered for a moment what Mo and the guys at the station would make of it: Carmen Dehan, the cop nobody wanted to work with because she had such a bad attitude.

After a while, the sobbing subsided and Elisa began to take deep, shaky breaths. She opened her eyes and put her hand over Dehan's again. "Thank you," she said. "I'm okay now. The Lord sends these trials to test us, but I know my Angela is with him, in Heaven." She braced herself and said, "You had better tell me what happened."

Dehan answered. "She was murdered, Mrs. Fernandez. I am so sorry . . ."

She shook her head. "I knew she would be. I told her not to go to New York. She was an innocent. I gave her my mother's cross to protect her. But it was no good. Please, don't tell me the details. I don't want to know. Just tell me, was it quick?"

I nodded and told a small, white lie. I said, "It was quick, Mrs. Fernandez, and she was unconscious."

"Thank the Lord for his mercy."

"Why was she in New York?"

She stared at the white tablecloth, at the place mat on which her glass was standing. For a moment I wondered if she had heard my question. Then she said, "She went to live with her boyfriend. I advised her not to. Father Byrne advised her not to also. But she said they were going to get married, just not yet. She told me not to worry, that everything was going to be okay."

Dehan took out her notebook and her pen. "What was her boyfriend's name, Mrs. Fernandez?"

"He was a local boy, Irish. Good boy, I liked him. Michael." She gave a small laugh. "The Irish have so many beautiful names, but they only ever use four! Sean, Patrick, Michael, and James." Her eyes drifted to the window. "Michael Shine. He was so in love with her. Every man who met her fell in love with her. She was so beautiful, and good and kind."

Dehan asked, "So Michael moved to New York?"

"He worked for a bank, here in Berwick. I can't remember which one. But he applied for a better job in New York, with a big bank, maybe HSBC, I can't remember. It wasn't a magnificent job, but for his age, you know, it was good. So he moved to New York."

I asked, "How long ago was this?"

"It was the beginning of March, 2016. And on April second she went to join him."

Dehan was frowning at her pad. "So let me be sure I have this right. Angela went to live with Michael in New York on April second, 2016?"

"That's correct." She nodded.

I scratched my head. "Is Michael still there?"

"Yes, he still writes to me, old-fashioned letters because I don't use a computer. At Christmas he comes to see me too."

"Could you give us his address? We are going to need to talk to him."

"935 C, Castle Hill Avenue. He has the top floor of one of

those big redbrick houses. She was very excited because it was next door to the public library, and she loved to read." She took a deep breath. "I am sorry, Detectives. This is very difficult for me. The thing is, she didn't stay with Michael. That is, she stayed with him for only about three weeks."

I was surprised and my face said so. "Oh?"

"Apparently she met somebody else. I am ashamed to admit it. It was certainly not the behavior I would have expected from her, and I am at a loss to explain it, but that is what happened. She moved out of Michael's apartment and moved in with this new man."

"Who was this new man, Mrs. Fernandez?"

"I have no idea."

I leaned forward, with my elbows on the table. "I want you to think very carefully, because this could be of vital importance. Is it possible that Michael was mistreating Angela? Was he hurting her? Is that why she moved out?"

"Oh, Lord no! Not at all. She said she felt very bad for him because he had been such a saint and a gentleman, but she had met another man and she had fallen head over heels in love with him. And he with her. And it would be wrong to stay with Michael when she felt that way about this other man . . ."

"A name, Mrs. Fernandez, she must have mentioned a name."

"She did, just a first name. She said she would write me with more details of her new address, and they would come and see me, but I never heard from her again."

Dehan said, "The name?"

She stared out the window for a long time. I was about to ask again, but she took another deep breath and looked down at the table, biting her lip. "I'll never forget the name as long as I live, but it makes me sick to my stomach to say it. Jimmy. The man who killed my daughter is called Jimmy."

TEN

WE LEFT HER A LITTLE WHILE LATER. SHE HAD CALLED friends who were going to come over and spend the evening with her. Dehan rested her ass on the hood of the Jag and pulled out her cell while I unlocked the door. She dialed and waited, squinting in the afternoon sun. After a moment she said, "Hey, Teddy, it's Detective Dehan, remember me?" She waited, sucking her teeth and looking up at the sky. "Yeah, okay, listen, Teddy . . ." He obviously kept talking because she paused, then repeated, "Teddy, listen to me. We really need that information. It has become a matter of extreme urgency, you understand me? I need to know Jimmy's last known address by tonight . . . Good, that's what I wanted to hear. You're a good man, Teddy. Bye."

I smiled as she opened the door and climbed in. "He was real busy," she said. Then she eyed me up and down. "It's looking like Jimmy, Sensei."

I turned the key and the engine roared into life. "It always did, Little Grasshopper. It always did." As we pulled away I said, "You want to call Shine and ask him to come in tomorrow? Early as he can. I want to talk to him before the DA arranges a deal for Wayne."

"You still think Wayne is our guy . . ."

"I don't think anything, Dehan. There are things about Wayne and his testimony that don't make sense." I smiled at her without rancor and added, "And honestly, I think the inspector, the DA, and you are jumping at the easy solution. There are things here that don't make sense, and I want them explained."

"Like the place where he says he was lying . . ."

"Amongst others. I'd also like to know why these girls kept falling in love and giving themselves body and soul to a guy who was, and I quote, 'not the sort of guy you'd notice.'" I glanced at her. "That from Pam and Teddy. Well, so far, this guy you wouldn't look twice at has got three attractive young ladies to A, fall out with her best friend so she could see him at the bar and then arrange to meet him Saturday instead of going home to Mom; B, spend a naughty weekend with him in the belief he could get her a job; and C, leave her boyfriend so she could move in with him because it was love at first sight. Now, I want you to tell me something, and I want you to be really honest."

"Oh God, what?"

"Wayne Harris, is he sexually fascinating?"

"No."

"Be honest, Dehan. I am not asking you, personally, if you find him attractive. I am talking in general. Has he got sexual magnetism?"

She sighed. "Okay, Stone, I guess to some women that kind of uninhibited, predatory bad boy stuff might be a turn-on."

"And he is intelligent enough to put himself across as a misunderstood good guy."

"Yes. But it still does not explain A, why he would implicate himself and B, as I keep telling you, he has no record of this kind of crime. You are fixating on him, Stone. What is it? Do you feel jealous or threatened by him?"

I raised an eyebrow at her. "Should I?"

"Good Lord, Stone! No!"

"Then I don't." I frowned. "Hey, we're investigating. We're

following the leads where they take us. Have I done anything unprofessional at any stage?"

"No. No you haven't, not at all. I'm sorry. I shouldn't have said that."

"What was the last thing I asked you to do?"

She sighed. "Call Shine."

"And what is the first thing I am going to ask him?"

She was beginning to look pissed. "I don't know Stone, what?"

"Seriously? What would you ask?"

"Where can we find Jimmy?"

"And that is what I am going to ask him. And as soon as we get the information from Teddy, we are going to see if they are in fact one and the same Jimmy. Is there anything irrational, negligent, or unprofessional about that plan?"

"No, Stone! Okay! You made your point!"

"So call."

She stared at me. I ignored her and after a moment she found the number and made the call. He agreed to come into the station first thing in the morning and she hung up. She stared out the window for ten minutes at the passing countryside, then said, "Stone, don't get mad at me. We don't get mad at each other."

I smiled at her. She smiled back. "I'm not mad at you, Dehan. Forget about us for a minute, be as objective as you can be, as a detective, an investigator, okay?" She nodded. "What made you ask me if I felt jealous or threatened?"

"C'mon, Stone! Let it go!"

"Be objective. You're not my . . . whatever you are. Just stand back and examine it. What made you ask that?"

She sighed and after a while she shook her head. "I don't know. It was a stupid question."

"You're still thinking like Carmen Dehan in love with the enigmatic and irresistible Detective John Stone."

"Yeah? Am I?"

"What made you ask it was that, unconsciously, you were

acknowledging that he is a very magnetic, sexual animal that is capable of seducing women and making men feel threatened. Something in which he is the polar opposite of Jimmy the barman."

I glanced at her. She was staring fixedly at the dashboard. After a while she nodded several times with her lips pursed. "Yup. You're right." She looked at me. "You can do that, can't you?"

"What?"

"Disconnect like that. Ignore your emotions. Be objective."

"Yes."

She thought about it, then said, "But I still think you're wrong. He's a scumbag, but he is not our guy. Maybe there are two Jimmies and the second one is irresistible. But Wayne is not the guy."

"Let's see where the evidence leads us, Carmencita."

And we drove on, into the gathering dusk.

———

MICHAEL SHINE WAS small and thin, with floppy blond hair and an agreeable face, and heels that tapped energetically when he walked. He wore a suit that was not expensive, but did not look cheap, and you could tell he had already decided at twenty-one exactly where he wanted to be at thirty-one. Now, at twenty-six, he was about halfway there and looking pleased with himself. As we came into the interrogation room he smiled without warmth and said, "I have to tell you, Detectives, right off, I haven't seen Angela, or heard from her, in over two years."

We sat opposite him and Dehan said, "Yeah, you guys broke up, right?"

He shook his head emphatically. "No. She broke up with me. I didn't break up with her."

She frowned. "Her mom told us you two were crazy about each other."

"That's what I thought. But the fact is you just don't know

people till you live with them, and even then you can't be sure. I wouldn't tell Elisa this because to her Angela was, well, just that, an angel. But the truth is, as soon as she arrived in New York she began to change. Seems she was only using me."

I said, "Using you for what?"

"To get away from home. Elisa is a sweet lady, but man!" He laughed. "She is really controlling!" He nodded several times, watching us, still smiling. "She is one controlling woman. You know? She'll have you sit at the dining table so you don't mess up the cushions on the couch. If you go to have dinner at her house, if she knows you at all, she'll have you eat in the kitchen so's not to mess the table. And that's just the tip of the iceberg. She controlled every aspect of Angela's life. And I guess that included me. Elisa wanted Angela to marry an Irish Catholic, so Angela picked me, took me home, got me approved by her mom, and right away started telling me we should move out of Berwick to New York."

Dehan leaned back in her chair. "So, you are telling me that Angela only moved in with you to get away from her mother."

"That's the way it seemed to me! I think we'd lived together for a week, maybe ten days, when I first noticed she was seeing another guy."

"How was that?"

"It was Saturday morning. I'd been to the gym. I usually have a good workout on Saturday morning." He gave a smile that was rueful and shook his head. "It'll show you what a sap I was. I was just starting my routine and I thought, 'What the hell! I got the most beautiful girl in the world, just moved in with me, and I'm working out at the gym? I'm going home, and I'm going to take her out for lunch in Manhattan!' See the sights. Have a magical day to remember. So I get in the car and I'm driving up Zerega, and I pass a bar, and who the hell do I see in the window, but Angela, sitting with a guy. Deep in conversation. You know, like they had a lot to talk about."

I said, "What did this guy look like?"

He shrugged. "Hard to say. It was fleeting and I was looking at her."

"So what happened?"

"Well, at that stage I was still crazy about her and trusted her. So I parked the car and called her, and I said, 'Baby, I'm not doing my workout today. I'm going to take you out on the town.' 'Oh, don't do that!' she says. 'Don't do that just for me. You need your workouts.' So I say, 'Well, I've already left. I'm at home. I'm just wondering what you're doing.' Because I'm beginning to think maybe there's something wrong. And she says, 'Well, I'm at the hairdresser. I won't be home for another hour at least.' And then I knew she was cheating on me."

Dehan asked him, "What did you do?"

"I said, 'Baby, I want you to come home right now 'cause I've got something real important I need to talk to you about.' And she could tell from my voice that it was serious. So she came right home. And I told her I had seen her at the bar and I had seen her with a man. And I wanted to know why she had lied to me, and who that man was."

I held up a hand. "Before we go on, Mr. Shine, what was the name of the bar?"

"Oh, Teddy's All-Night Bar."

"And the man you had seen her with, was this Jimmy?"

"That's what she said. She said she only lied because she didn't think I would understand. There was nothing romantic or sexual between them. He was just offering her a job."

I frowned. "What kind of job?"

"Some kind of bullshit about production assistant in a production company. They got talking when she went there for a pizza at lunchtime one day. They got talking, she said she was looking for a job . . . I don't need to tell you how it goes."

Dehan said, "So what happened?"

"What happened was that I told her she was naïve, and that I didn't want her seeing this guy anymore, and I didn't want her going to bars on her own, even at lunchtime. She promised but you know how it is, once you start suspecting, it's real hard to shake it. So a couple of times I made an excuse at work and drove around the area. And it was maybe a week or ten days after I saw her in the bar, I saw her there again. Only this time they were holding hands. I felt sick. You can imagine. I waited till she came out and I followed her. She went home. I went up after her and I told her, 'I saw you at the bar with that guy. You were holding hands. What's going on?' She told me they'd met a few times, they'd fallen in love. It was just one of those things. She was sorry and she was moving in with him."

I drummed my fingers on the table. "Did she tell you anything else about him?"

"Yeah. It was his dad's company. It was called Directed Vision or something like that. They had a contract with NBC and he was going to fix her up there with a job and she was going to study TV production while she worked."

"Did she tell you his last name?"

His gaze became abstracted. He stared at the wall. "Yeah. I remember I thought it was a stupid name for a producer, because it was like film more, get it?"

"Jimmy Fillmore?"

He nodded. "Yeah. Stupid. She didn't see it."

Dehan asked him, "Did she give you an address where she was going?"

"Not exactly. We parted on really bad terms, as you can imagine. She told me she wanted to stay till Saturday, because he had something going on at his house till Saturday. Then she could move in with him. I told her to take a hike, so she stayed a few days with a couple we were friends with, and I never heard from her again."

"We're going to need an address for your friends."

He was beginning to frown. "Sure, Ai Hitani and Bill Walters, 1717 Yates Avenue." He gave her Ai's number. "Say, what is this about? What has Angela done?"

I nodded. "Mr. Shine, the second time you saw Angela with this Jimmy Fillmore, did you get a better look at him?"

He sat back and thought. "Yeah, I guess. Maybe midtwenties, dark hair. It looked black, but hard to tell for sure. He might have been Hispanic, or Italian, but not real dark. They were sitting down most of the time, but when she left he stood to give her a kiss. She was five three or four. I guess he was less than a foot taller. So maybe he was six foot. Not big, normal build." He looked at Dehan, then looked back at me. "What is this about?"

"Mr. Shine, Angela was murdered that Saturday, not far from the bar where you saw her, by the river. Do you recall the Westchester Angel?"

"Holy shit! That was *Angela*?"

Dehan was frowning at him. "You weren't struck by the similarities? The location, the crucifix . . ."

He was shaking his head. "I had no idea. I never have time to watch the news. I read the financial pages. I don't know anything about a crucifix. She had one, belonged to her grandmother . . ."

I nodded. "That was Angela, Mr. Shine."

He had gone very pale and his hand had started shaking. "Jesus, if I had known I would have never . . . She was with friends. It wasn't as if I put her on the street. I would never have . . . if I'd known."

"There was no way you could have known. You can't blame yourself. She had made her choice. What we have to do is catch the man who did it to her."

He stared at me with big, unseeing eyes. "Jimmy," he said. "Jimmy Fillmore did it."

"That is what we aim to find out," I said, half to myself, as he and Dehan stood. She showed him to the door and he left.

ELEVEN

I pulled out my cell and started to dial. I glanced at Dehan. She was standing by the door. I said, "What's the deal with Teddy? He's dragging his heels. Why don't you give him a call and lean on him a bit?"

She nodded and stepped out of the room, pulling her phone from her pocket. My number rang twice and an attractive voice said, "Hello?"

"Ms. Ai Hitani?"

"Speaking. Who is this please?"

"This is Detective John Stone of the New York Police Department. Can you spare me a couple of minutes to talk about Angela Fernandez?"

There was a moment's silence, then her voice again with a frown in it. "Angela? Sure. Is she okay?"

"Ms. Hitani, I believe Angela stayed with you for a few days a couple of years back, after she broke up with Michael."

"Yes, she did, that's right."

"Do you know where she went after that?"

Another silence. "Um, yes, she moved in with her boyfriend. Well, her new boyfriend. We were all a little startled that she had switched so suddenly, but she seemed pretty swept off her feet."

"Do you recall his name?"

"Yeah, sure, Jimmy something."

"Did you hear from her after that?"

"No, we never did."

"Did she give you an address?"

"No. He called, came and picked her up, and we never heard from her again. We weren't real close. We were more Mike's friends. Is she okay?"

I sighed. "No, I'm afraid she has been murdered." There was a small gasp at the other end of the phone. I went on, "Ms. Hitani, Angela was murdered that Saturday. We have reason to believe that whoever picked her up was responsible for her death. Someone will be around later to take a statement from you and from Mr. Walters. In the meantime, please try to remember anything you can about what she said to you about her new boyfriend."

She said she would, and I hung up. Dehan was leaning on the doorjamb, watching me. "He was falling over himself with apologies. He was looking for it right there and then. I told him I didn't want to have to charge him with withholding evidence. He swore he was on it. He knows he has it, he just can't remember exactly where."

"Good. Maybe we should go help him look."

"On the other hand, we have Angela's phone and bank records."

I nodded. "Okay. I'm going to start going through her phone records, see who she spoke to on Friday and Saturday. Meantime, you want to go and take a statement from Ai Hitani and Bill Walters?"

Her eyes flicked over my face for a second. "Sure." She paused. I stood. She said, "You okay, Stone?"

"Never better. Let's go."

I gave her the keys to the Jag and we went downstairs.

The bank and phone records were on my desk. There was only one thing I was interested in, and I leafed through the phone records until I found it. Friday and Saturday, the 13th and 14th of May, 2016. There were not many calls: a couple out of state to Pennsylvania, and a cell phone that called her late Friday and just before midnight. It lasted ten minutes, and then called again Saturday at two p.m.

I dialed the number. It rang three times and was answered by a woman who sounded flustered. "Yes? Who is this?"

"This is Detective John Stone of the NYPD, ma'am, who am I speaking to?"

"This is Mrs. Silvia Sterling. What do you want?"

"Mrs. Sterling, how long have you had this number?"

"Are you serious? Is this some kind of joke?"

"No, ma'am, it is not a joke. It is part of a homicide inquiry. If you like, you can call the Forty-Third Precinct and ask for Detective John Stone, they'll put you through to me. However, it would save time if you simply told me how long . . ."

"Yes, all right! I have had this number for about a year. Do you need the exact date?"

"No, thank you, ma'am. That is all I needed to know. You have a good day."

I hung up and called AT&T and asked them to tell me who had that telephone number in May of 2016. They said it would take time and I went upstairs to talk to Inspector John Newman. When I knocked and went in, he didn't look real pleased to see me.

"John." He sighed and gestured at the chair opposite him. "Come in, sit down. You look troubled."

I nodded. "I'm not happy about the deal with Wayne Harris."

"I know you have reservations, John."

"It's more than reservations, sir. I have real concerns."

He spread his hands. "All right, let's hear them."

I thought for a moment. "For a start, we don't need him. We are closing in on a prime suspect, Jimmy Fillmore . . ."

"Have you got an address?"

"Not yet."

"A photograph so we can put out an APB?"

"No, not yet . . ."

"National Insurance number? Anything more than a name?"

"Not yet, sir."

He studied my face for a moment, then said, "What are your other concerns?"

"Wayne's story, about how he was at the river and witnessed Angela's murder, it just doesn't hold up for me."

"Why not?"

"For a start, I went and lay down on the spot where he said he was lying, smoking a joint and gazing at the stars, when the killer showed up." I shook my head. "He wasn't lying there. You couldn't. It was covered in stones and prickly bushes. When we took him there, to find Angela's purse, he didn't know the path to that location: he knew the path to the spot where Angela was killed. Also, he needed to get up close to the spot where her purse was buried, and then he knew the exact spot. That is not consistent with someone who saw it concealed from almost a hundred yards away—in the dark."

He nodded. "They are all good points, and classic John Stone, insightful thinking. But it is not . . . *substantial* enough to warrant stopping the deal. We have a serial killer out there, John. It was your own intuitive brilliance that found him . . ."

"Sir, my gut tells me that Wayne Harris has developed a dangerous fixation on Detective Dehan. If he is released on the strength of this deal, she could be seriously at risk."

He grunted and looked down at his thumbs, as though he was trying to decide which one he liked best. "You believe Wayne could be our killer and he is playing a deep game?"

"I don't know, but what I do know is that whenever she has been present at an interview with him, she has had to withdraw from the conversation because he cannot focus when she is present."

He frowned at me. "What do you mean?"

I sighed again. "He fixates. He seems to believe that he and

Detective Dehan have some kind of special connection. He began talking about the primal drives of the deep unconscious that united them. It was not good stuff to listen to, sir."

"It is natural that you should feel protective toward her. She is your partner in more senses than one . . ."

I fought to keep the irritation from my voice. "Sir, I would feel the same way if he was talking this way about Maria Sanchez at the local grocery store. He was unquestionably present at Angela's murder, he knew the exact location of her purse, and he is fixating on a young woman who fits the model of our killer's victims. That for me is a pretty powerful reason to stop the deal."

He closed his eyes and pinched the bridge of his nose. "You understand that this is a very difficult call, Stone."

I shook my head and said simply, "No."

There was irritation in his eyes when he opened them. "All right, let's look at it this way. Suppose we talk to Wayne, he gives us the name of the alleged killer, and it does not pan out. It leads to nothing. Then he stays where he is in prison and you are free to continue your investigation into either this James Fillmore *or* Wayne Harris." He shrugged. "However, if, on the other hand, the information he gives us is good and we catch the man responsible, then we have taken a serial killer off the streets and you have your assurance that Wayne Harris is not the man and, in all probability, he is not fixating on Carmen but merely having a bit of fun at your expense."

"A bit of fun?"

"Forgive me, I didn't mean to sound flippant, but you take my meaning. It is reprehensible, but not life-threatening."

I raised an eyebrow at him, stared out the window a moment, then looked back at him. "All I am asking is for a little more time."

He shook his head. "It's no longer in my hands, John. It's with the DA. The decision will be taken, in all probability this afternoon, by the state. It is out of our hands." I made to stand. "John, I know your track record and there is not another detective whom I respect more than you, but you should know that the DA is adamant that we need this deal, and he has asked me to form a task force to go through all the Jane Does found in the river in the last five years, to see how many we can attribute to this killer. When the press get a hold of it, it could blow up in our faces, accusations of negligence, of racial bias, if they had been white girls this would not have happened . . ." He gestured at me. "I don't need to tell you. You know the way it goes. They want it wrapped up before any of that happens. If Wayne is on the level, he will get his deal this afternoon."

I knew he was right. I nodded. "Okay, thank you, sir."

I left his office and went slowly down the stairs. I sat for twenty minutes at my desk staring at empty space and going over every aspect of the case in my mind. It was like a jigsaw where you have all the corners and the edges, but the stuff in the middle belongs to a different puzzle. Three such similar girls, each from a different state, come together in such a small geographical area, all murdered one Saturday after another. Most serial killers are stalkers, but this didn't seem to be the result of stalking. What was it the result of?

Dehan came in, dropped into her chair, put her feet on the desk, and tossed me my keys. "Nothing more than what she told you already. She was at home with her husband and her kid. She works from home, he's a househusband, and the kid is . . . well, remind me not to have kids unless either they are mute or I go deaf." She sighed. "They promised to discuss it tonight when little Izamu Augustus Hitani-Walters, with a hyphen, was asleep. They will then open a bottle of French wine and talk about Angela's visit and see if anything comes to mind. We are grateful to them, Stone. Be grateful."

I nodded but didn't smile. "I am."

"You still worried?"

I did more nodding. "Yup, and the more I go over it in my mind, the more worried I become. We are rats in a maze, Dehan. We are being driven down a path to an unavoidable conclusion."

"I don't know what to say, Stone. We have to follow the

evidence and right now Wayne Harris' testimony is part of the evidence. It's practically the only evidence we've got that we *can* follow. I don't see we have much choice."

"My point exactly, Dehan. I couldn't have put it better myself." She frowned at me, hard, like she thought I was losing my grip. Just to compound her doubts I added, "I have a very bad feeling. Something bad is going to happen, and I don't know how to stop it. We are sitting here with a triple homicide—at least—and not a single clue to go on until the DA gives us the go-ahead with Wayne."

She made a face that said she didn't know what the hell had got into me. "So, thank heavens for Wayne, right?"

"Yeah, precisely."

"C'mon, Stone! If the information is bad, he gets no deal. If it's good, we have nothing to worry about. Stop worrying for crying out loud!"

Before I could answer the internal phone rang.

"John, it's me, the inspector. We have the go-ahead from the DA. I have had the deal printed and I'm sending it down to you now. She stressed upon me that this is something that needs to be cleared up in short order."

I tried to smile and failed. "With all due respect to the Powers that Be, sir, I am more motivated by the next potential victim than by their political anxieties."

"Of course, of course, I agree with you. John, about your own personal anxieties, if you want somebody else . . . perhaps Detective Dehan . . ."

"No. I can handle it, sir."

"Good. Good. Glad to hear it. You know where we stand."

"I am very clear on that, sir."

"Good, good," he said again. "Well, go get 'em!"

He hung up. I sighed noisily at Dehan. "We have the green light. The deal is on its way down."

She shrugged. "I'm sorry, Stone, but I'm glad. Let's get this son of a bitch and put him away."

A uniform came in with a manila folder and handed it to me. "From the inspector, Detective Stone."

I thanked him and he went away. I had just started to read when the internal phone buzzed again. Dehan picked it up. She was very quiet and that made me look up. She was making a note on a piece of paper. After a moment she said, "Okay, thanks," and hung up. She looked at me and there was something almost apologetic in her expression. "They found another body."

I threw the file on the desk. I had a hot knot of anger burning in my belly. "Goddamn it!" I grabbed my keys and stood. "Where is it? Ferry Point Park?"

She was halfway to her feet and froze. "How could you possibly know that?"

"It's called common sense!" I said savagely and stormed out of the station.

She grabbed her jacket and the folder and came running after me. "Slow down there, Sensei! What the hell is that supposed to mean?"

I climbed in the car and slammed the door. She got in the other side and I fired up the engine. She stared at me as I backed out. "Stone! You want to explain?"

"I've been explaining!" I snapped. I rammed in first, looked at her, and said, "Remember I said something bad was going to happen and I couldn't stop it? Well this is it!"

TWELVE

THE BODY WAS IN THE WOODS, ON THE EAST SIDE OF the freeway, where it borders the mouth of the creek. Frank and the crime scene team were already there when we arrived, and the uniforms had cordoned off the area with yellow tape, suspended like bunting from tree to tree. She was Hispanic, about twenty-two, lying on her back in a small clearing, looking up at the sky through the canopy above. Her elbows were bent and her hands were on her chest, bound with a silk handkerchief. She had a short skirt that had been pulled up around her hips, and her legs were splayed. She had no panties. There was bruising around her mouth and neck, and a big, ugly black bruise on her windpipe. Frank was squatting by her side. He glanced at us but didn't say anything.

I asked, "Is it the same MO?"

"I don't want to commit myself to anything at this stage, John, but I can tell you it is very similar. You can see for yourself . . ." He gestured at the handkerchief, at the skirt.

"ID?"

"No purse. We'll run her prints back at the lab."

I nodded and looked across the stretch of parkland toward the river. The water was concealed by the trees that bordered the banks. I walked away from the body, out onto the grass, and looked north toward where we'd left the car, then south toward the East River and the Whitestone Bridge. Dehan came and joined me, squinting in the sun and tying her hair behind her neck. "What are you thinking?"

I didn't look at her. I was scanning the area. I said, "Clearly Wayne couldn't have done it because he was in prison. Alibis don't come much better than that, right? So I'm wondering how the killer arrived." I pointed north. He either came down the Hutchinson River Parkway, left his car on the wasteland there, and then came down into the woods along the path, on foot . . ."

She nodded. "Or he drove all the way down to the bridge and came in that way."

She thought about it a moment. "If he came in via the bridge late at night there's less risk of being seen."

I watched her face, nodded, then shook my head. "Nope, because that road is cut off with big, steel gates. His only access is on foot."

She narrowed her eyes. "So . . . ?"

"So he must have driven here, left his car in the parking lot, and brought her to the woods here on foot. That make sense to you?"

She shrugged. "I can't see how he could do it any other way."

"Neither can I."

She looked unhappy and tense. "I feel like you're making a point and I don't know what it is. Am I missing something?"

"Not making a point. Just examining the new evidence, Dehan. We are all missing something in this case." I turned and pointed again, back along the path. "So, what is that? Five hundred yards?"

She looked and nodded. "Yeah, about that."

I walked back in among the trees. Frank was getting to his feet and they were loading the body onto a gurney. I had a closer look at her. Her face was bloated and distorted, and her cheeks were stained with mascara where she had been weeping. Her lipstick was smeared where her killer had been kissing her, the way Wayne had described it. I looked at her blouse. It was a white halter-neck made from some synthetic imitation silk. Where it had been ripped you could make out a bra that probably came from Victoria's Secret.

Frank pulled off his gloves. "You don't need to say anything, John. I've already had the call. This takes priority over everything."

I said, "She's been raped. You'll find semen inside her, also on her skirt, but you won't find any prints."

Dehan approached. "She's not wearing panties. Maybe he took them as a trophy."

"Yeah, maybe."

Frank spread his hands. "At the moment it is all speculation until I get back to the lab. I'll call you as soon as I know something."

I shoved my hands in my pockets and started walking back toward the car. Dehan fell into step beside me. "Stone, you know something?"

"Not much."

"You're being a pain in the ass."

"I'm sorry."

"Talk to me."

"I've been talking to you, Dehan."

She stopped dead in her tracks and gestured back toward the crime scene with her open hand. "Come on, Stone!"

"'Come on, Stone' is not a persuasive argument, Dehan. What are you trying to tell me?"

She jabbed several times with her hand. "You yourself have been saying that our killer may have been killing for a long time and may still be killing. This is not a copycat. Nobody knows his MO. You want it to be Wayne, Stone, but it *can't be!*"

I smiled.

"What are you smiling at?"

"You. You said you wanted me to talk to you, but actually it was you who wanted to talk to me. You have made your point. The inspector, the DA, and the State of New York all agree with you. So let's go and see who Wayne Harris tells us the killer is."

"Like I said, you're being a pain in the ass!"

She marched on ahead and then had to sit on the hood and wait for me to arrive. As I arrived and pulled out my keys, she said, "I just don't get why you have to play this blame game."

I frowned at her, opened the door, and got in.

She got in the passenger seat and slammed the door. "I am not betraying you just because I don't agree with you!"

I pulled out of the lot and headed toward the Expressway.

After a moment she said, "You don't have to guilt-trip me. I can have a different opinion from you. I don't have to agree with you all the time."

After I had turned west onto the Bruckner Expressway, she looked at me and said, "Aren't you going to say anything?"

I glanced at her and sighed. "What do you want me to say, Dehan? You're mad at me. I am not mad at you. You have a different opinion from me. That's fine. I haven't got time to argue with you. I am trying to figure out how to avoid another woman getting killed, and that is taking up all of my attention. I'm sorry you feel I'm guilt-tripping you, but I do not feel betrayed."

After a bit she said, "You don't?"

"No."

Her phone rang. She pulled it from her pocket and answered, "Dehan."

She listened, glanced at me, looked embarrassed, and said, "Yes, sir, Frank is giving it priority. He'll get back to us as soon as he has anything." She was silent again. "It seems to have been the same killer, yes, sir. The MO is the same." Another silence. "We are on our way to Rikers now. Yes, sir, I understand. We will, sir . . . . He is right here beside me, sir. He's driving. Yes, I'll tell him, sir."

"That was . . ."

"I know who it was."

"He wanted . . ."

"I know what he wanted. He wanted to make sure I didn't sabotage the deal. Do you want to take the lead in this investigation, Dehan?"

Her eyes went wide. "No! *John!*"

"Are you sure?"

"Of course I'm sure!"

"Do you think the inspector would like you to take over?"

"No! John, stop it!"

"Perhaps you should ask him."

"John, you are having a tantrum like a spoiled kid!"

I smiled at her. "If you and he don't approve of my conduct of the inquiry, then perhaps you should lead. It's not a big deal, Dehan."

She folded her arms and didn't talk to me again until we reached the prison. When I parked the car in the lot, I climbed out and called the inspector. He sounded embarrassed.

"Stone, what can I do for you?"

"Is there anything you need to say to me, sir?"

"Um, no, just, ah . . . what I said to Carmen, um, you were driving."

"Do I still have the lead on this case, sir?"

"Of course you do, Stone! Naturally . . ."

"Thank you, sir."

I hung up. Dehan was staring at me, shaking her head. "You're being ridiculous."

I pulled my laptop from the back seat and closed the door, then stared at her for a long moment. I handed her the key and said, "Dehan, will you please go to Teddy's Late-Night Bar and, if you have to drag him by his collar and put a gun to his head, make him give you Jimmy Fillmore's details."

"Are you kidding me?"

"No. And the instant he gives them to you, call me."

"Stone, are you serious? Are you sidelining me?"

I stepped toward her. "Dehan, this is important. For one thing, Wayne cannot concentrate when you are in his presence.

For another, if we get Jimmy Fillmore before Wayne talks, we don't need the deal. And whatever you think of my instincts, you will at least admit that Wayne Harris is one son of a bitch who should not be on the street."

She blinked at me.

"But more than that, Dehan, if you have ever known my gut to be right, then please give it the benefit of the doubt now. I am not sidelining you. I am asking you to do something important. More important than wasting time on this stupid deal."

She blinked at me again.

I felt a knot of hot anger in my gut. "Carmen, I am asking you to do what I would be doing if I didn't have to be here. Please do it!"

She snatched the keys from me and climbed in the car. I watched her pull out of the lot and accelerate away. Then I turned toward the prison complex and started to walk.

———

THE CLANG and roll of the steel doors echoed down concrete corridors like a clumsy death knell. Wayne was brought in, manacled and shuffling in his orange jumpsuit. He smiled his snake-smile at me as he crossed the floor and sat at the table. His guards cuffed him. He watched me as the officers left the room and slammed the door shut. My laptop was set up to record the conversation. He watched me press Record and smiled.

"I really scared Detective Dehan, huh?"

"Is that something you enjoy, Wayne, scaring women?"

He sighed, like a man who has grown tired of a game. "You got me all wrong, Detective Stone." I waited while he studied my face a little longer. "I know I am my own worst enemy. My momma was always tellin' me that: 'Wayne Harris, you are your own worst enemy!' My daddy never told me nothin'. He just took his belt to me on a regular basis." He gave a small laugh. "You might say that he made me strong and she gave me self-awareness."

I yawned loudly. "Is this going somewhere, Wayne?"

"Yeah, it's goin' somewhere, Detective. I'm tellin' you why you got me all wrong."

"Who killed Angela Fernandez?"

He laughed. "Whoa there, boy! Buy a girl a drink! Give me a chance!"

"No. I'm getting bored, Wayne. I don't believe you know jack. I think you're a narcissistic asshole who likes to play games, and you get off on all the attention you get from pretending you know something about this killer. Now I don't give a damn about your momma and your daddy back in Arizona. I want to know who killed Angela Fernandez. Do you know or not?"

It was odd. Very little changed about his face: a slight lowering of his lids, a hardening of an already granite expression, but the effect was powerful. Just for a moment, there was murderous hatred in his expression, but it passed.

"Yeah, Stone, I know who killed Angela, and I know a lot more besides. And we are going to do this my way, or not at all. And the longer you delay, the more bodies you are going to have on your list." He sat forward and narrowed his eyes at me. "I have a lot of shit on my conscience, Stone. A lot of bad shit. But I don't belong in this fuckin' hellhole. I aim to get out, but when I get out it will be righteous. You understand that concept, Stone? When I get out I ain't comin' back. And that means I have to be clean in here . . ." He went to thump his chest with his fist but the cuffs jarred him.

I snarled at him, "Talk to a priest. I'm a cop, not your confessor!"

He snarled back, "And that's why it's got to be you!" He sat back. "You listen to me, tell it my way or you can fuck off back to your inspector and your fuckin' DA with empty fuckin' hands. Your choice."

I raised an eyebrow at him. "Talk, but cut to the chase at some point, will you?" To underline the point I dropped the folder with the agreement in it on the table where he couldn't reach it. "I've done worse things in my life than go back to the inspector and the DA with empty hands. And for the record, my personal opinion is that this shithole is exactly where you belong, so don't push me, Wayne, because the final decision is mine."

He waited a moment, then asked, "You done?"

"Talk."

He waited a moment, then seemed to sag. "I came in here today with the intention of makin' you see that I ain't the man you think I am." He tried to raise his hands. "Don't come back with some wisecrack, Stone, just listen, okay?

"But you just wind me up, you know? Like one of them toys you used to get where you turned a key and they started doin' all kinds of crazy things. I just look at you and I want to fuck with your head."

I waited.

He stared at me, then took a deep breath. "But, that's what I was trying to tell you. It's what my momma used to tell me. I am my own worst enemy." He looked around him at the walls for a moment. "You know what I used to do when my daddy would come in and say to me, 'Wayne, did you cut the head off of your sister's doll?' or 'Wayne, you been smokin' in the barn again?' or 'Wayne, have you been drinkin' my whiskey?'"

He waited, as though he expected me to answer. Finally I sighed. "No, Wayne, what did you do?"

"I never did none of those things, man. Smokin' in the barn is plumb stupid, because the hay can catch fire, right? I don't like whiskey, never did. I drink rum, and not much of that. And you won't never catch Wayne Harris playin' with dolls, even to cut off their fuckin' heads. Besides, I loved my little sister. No, it was my brother Earl who done all them things. But when my daddy used to ask me, I answered him with all the fuckin' insolence I knew how. I knew he was gonna whip me, but I didn't care. I told him, 'You ain't never gonna cow me, you motherfucker.' And he never did. But my momma would say to me, 'Wayne, you are your own worst enemy.' And in that sense she was right, because I would bring on myself punishment I didn't deserve, just for the sake of being contrary, and not bowin' to the man with the whip. Now you come in here, with all your fuckin' authority, and I just want to make you mad." He paused, smiling his snake-smile. "And I knew soon as I looked at you, one thing that really makes you mad is an animal like me messin' with your lady, am I right?"

"Are we done with the confessional?"

"Almost."

He sat for a long while looking at his hands cuffed on the table. He sat so long I started to think of getting up and leaving, but finally he started talking again. He was serious; he didn't look at me and he had lost his mocking tone. It was almost like talking to a different person.

"I'm a hard case, Detective Stone. I been in my fair share of brawls, I smoked a lot of dope and I sold a lot of dope, and I snorted my fair share of coke." He raised his eyes to look at me. "But I ain't a criminal. I never killed nobody and I never stole from nobody who wasn't a thief. I'm a pain in the ass, I know that, and I'm a contrary son of a bitch. But seriously, with this body, and my attitude, if I was of a true criminal disposition, don't you think I'd have a real rap sheet by now? Only reason I'm in prison, Detective, is because New York has stupid laws on drugs. Anywhere else in this country I'd be out on the street by now." He hesitated, looked away, looked mad. "So, I'm sorry I came on to Detective Dehan. It was a stupid thing to do, but I couldn't help myself."

I considered him for a while until he turned his head to look at me again. Then I said, "Apology accepted. Now, do you know who killed Angela Fernandez?"

He nodded. "Oh, yeah," he said, and his face went hard. "I know who that son of a bitch is."

THIRTEEN

"Here's the way I see it, Stone." He sat forward and put his elbows on the table. "The State of New York has stolen my freedom. Now I want my freedom back." He nodded his head toward the folder. "If that is the offer you have for me, then we can talk turkey."

I pushed the folder in front of him and opened it so he could read the document inside it. "You give me the name of Angela's killer, and if the evidence you give is probative of his guilt, or leads to his conviction, your sentence will be reduced to time served. That is as good as you are going to get."

"It's good enough," he said without looking at me, and continued to read the document in minute detail. When he had finished, he sat back in his chair and took a deep breath. Then he smiled.

"I'm a drifter, Stone, what you might call a bum. I traveled all over this great country of ours. I like the South. I like the Southwest. A man can be free down there. And in Wyoming. Up here in the Northeast, man, this is like the Illuminati control everything, you feel me? But I kind of arrived here, three years ago, to do a bit of business which does *not* concern you . . ." He wheezed his rasping laugh. "And I don't know, man, I just kind of stayed. I don't know why, I like the Bronx, or I did back then. It was kind of rebellious, know what I'm sayin'? People are free here, you know? They kick against the yoke. I like that. But I don't like it over yonder, Hunts Point, over the river, man, Longwood, that's not my scene. Like I keep tellin' you. I ain't a criminal, I am just anarchic. I don't like no man tellin' me what I cannot do. So I found myself a pad near Castle Hill Avenue, south of the expressway. I read there was a real low crime rate there. I could feel easy and at peace. I like that." He leered. "I could feel like a nice, middle-class gentleman, just like my momma wanted me to be. You know what I'm sayin'?"

I looked at my watch and sighed.

"Don't be rude, Detective Stone. If I get upset I may have to ask you to come back tomorrow."

"Keep going. I'm listening."

"'I'm listening.' Who used to say that, man? I like that. 'I'm listening.'"

"Dr. Frasier Crane."

He laughed. "That's right. I used to like that. A nice American family, human, but fundamentally driven by good American values. Big Brother is watching, Dr. Frasier Crane is listening. I like that."

"Deep. So what happened?"

"I found me a nice bar I could frequent. They was good times for me. I was makin' a bit of money, I read the *New York Times* over breakfast, and I frequented a nice neighborhood bar in the evening, as a middle-class gentleman should. There ain't a lot of nice bars around Castle Hill and Zerega, did you know that?"

"So you frequented Teddy's Late-Night Bar."

"You are a veritable Sherlock Holmes, Detective Stone. That is exactly the bar I settled on. I was happy, and I started to re-create myself, far away from the pernicious influence of my father and his belt." He paused. "You know what? I am fundamentally a very positive kind of man. Since I been locked up in this hellhole, I have been using my time constructively. I have been seeing a therapist, I have been reading the classics, and I have been studying the essays of Sigmund Freud, so that I can better understand my own, unconscious motivations."

"I'm impressed. So you started hanging out at Teddy's. Is that where you developed your obsession with Hispanic girls, or did you have that from before?"

He laughed a laugh that sounded like somebody rasping through volcanic rock. "You're smart, Stone, but not as smart as you think you are. I have no interest in Hispanic babes. Your boy does. My only reason for hitting on your Carmen Dehan was to rile you."

"So your interest was in me, not her."

"You could say that. Call it an unresolved Oedipal complex. You remind me of my dad. My mom? She was pretty as a picture, pale skin, freckles, Scandinavian hair so blond it was almost white, and blue, blue eyes. Hard as fuckin' nails. But a good, Christian woman. Your made-in-a-mold, standard Latina beauty don't do much for me. They all look the same, know what I'm sayin'?"

"So who's my man?"

"So I used to go there two or three nights in the week, have myself a rum or two with my beer, read the paper and sometimes a book. And in time I got to know some of the patrons and made friends. Sometimes Teddy and I would discuss the issues of the day. He ain't no genius, but he can hold a good conversation and, what is most important, he is a law-abidin' citizen who does not allow antisocial elements into his bar. His bar is strictly for decent, middle-class folks who don't want no trouble. That was, and is, what I aspire to be."

I raised an eyebrow and he sighed and closed his eyes. "Dr. Mack tells me that one of the ways I sabotage myself is that when I talk from the heart, I make myself out to be some kind of clown. Like I am mocking myself. Like I don't even believe me." He opened his eyes. "He says that is a defense mechanism."

"Really?"

"Yeah, really."

"So you made friends at Teddy's Late-Night Bar. What happened next?"

"He had this boy workin' for him. He looked Latino himself." He shook his head. "No, not Latino. Because, you know? There is a difference. Latinos are like more South American, and they have Indian—Native American—blood in them. They are more beautiful, you feel me? Their skin is darker and smoother, their eyes are deeper, their hair is blacker. Hispanic, the word comes from *España*, and the Spanish are more mixed. They have more European blood in them. There were Celts living in Spain, and Goths and Basques. You get a lot of blond Spaniards, did you know that? And a lot of Spaniards have real pale skin." He pointed at me with his manacled hands. "Those that have dark skin, that is Arab blood, not Native American. It's a different skin altogether, man. They are like Italians and Greek. Not beautiful at all."

I nodded. "Okay."

"So, this kid was more Hispanic than Latino. Black hair, big brown eyes, he could have been a . . ." He grinned. "He could have been a Corleoni, or a Gambini, you know what I'm sayin' to you?"

"But he wasn't."

"Uh-uh. This kid's name was like yours, Stone, of English origin. Mine, mine is Scottish. Are you interested in the etymology of names, Stone?"

"No, not really, and you're clowning again. Get to the point, Wayne."

He winked without smiling, pointed a finger at me like a gun from a manacled wrist, and made a "Tsk!" sound. "You got me." He was serious for a bit, thinking. "Let me tell it my way, Detective Stone. You're getting what you want. You know . . . ?" He nodded a few times, then shrugged. "Maybe, if you listen, you might get something extra."

"Fine, keep going. He wasn't Italian Mafia."

"No, he wasn't that, though if the mood took him he might

have told you he was. Here's the thing about that boy. He was always tellin' you stories. His mom was a Mexican hooker from Los Angeles. His daddy was a film star." He laughed. "He'd never tell you who, you know what I'm sayin'? But he'd leave you clues, like, real obvious clues—like, he'd tell you what movies he starred in." He threw back his head and laughed out loud. "Sometimes it was Robert De Niro, sometimes it was Al Pacino, one time it was George Clooney, and that I could almost believe, you know? He kind of looked like George Clooney . . . them big eyes."

He chuckled. I waited.

"He was a liar. A *big* liar. He could not help himself. Me and Ted, we would laugh and joke about it. He never did nobody any harm with his stories. He was just a dreamer and he could not tell the difference half the time 'tween what was a daydream and what was real." He settled his ass in the chair. "But see, I think that's where the problem was. 'Cause, I told you this was kind of like a family bar. During the day all kinds of people would come in and have some lunch, or a coffee. It was a nice place. And see, he had an eye for nice, Catholic Latinas. I used to make fun of him sometimes and he didn't like it. Used to make him mad. I'd tell him, 'I see you, looking at that girl. She's too good for you, boy. She's gonna be a doctor, or an attorney.'" He shook his head. "Then he'd go off on one of his fantasies. He was studyin' night school to be a film director, and his famous daddy was gonna help him. He was just workin' at the bar to pay for his classes . . .'" He shook his head again. "Man, I guess it was pretty sad."

I drew breath to ask him about his delusions about being a filmmaker, but he raised a finger and shook his head. "Let me tell it my way, Mr. Stone. You'll get everything you want. You have my word." He licked his lips and took a deep breath through his nose, looking up at the ceiling. "So, I began to notice, because, believe it or not, Stone, I am an observer of human conduct. I began to *observe* that in the evenings, and sometimes during the day, he would approach certain girls, always the same kind of girls, pretty Latinas, always kind of what you might call *demure*: nice, polite, well-dressed. They would always keep to theirselves, drink maybe a glass of white wine, never get drunk. You know the kind of nice, Catholic girl I am talkin' about. And I do believe that he fell in love with each and every one of them. They would ignore him to begin with, but he'd come across as inoffensive, a bit naïve, you know what I'm sayin'? And before you knew it he was tellin' them his stories and they was wanting to mother him, because all nice Catholic girls just wanna be mothers, you know? They want to be the Virgin Mary. It's an archetype thing, you feel me?"

"I feel you, dude. So what happened?"

"So one night he's talking to these two chicks, only one of them is Latina, the other is a white chick. And the Latina is suckin' it up, man. He's tellin' her his daddy is George Clooney and all that shit . . ." He wheezed his laugh, leaning forward and shaking his head. "And she is buyin' it, man. And, you know what? The next night she comes back alone, and dude, the son of a bitch is hitting on her big-time and she is into him, man! I never knew he had it in him. I see him do it a couple of times. And I told Ted, you know? 'Man, Ted, respect for this kid! He's getting more pussy than I am, dude!'"

He paused and became serious again. "It was, ahh . . . Saturday night, May fourteenth. I'd been havin' a few beers and a couple of rums at Teddy's, and I know he don't like people smokin' there, even outside dude, especially if you're smokin' weed, know what I'm sayin'? But I knew there was this nice place down by the river, where I took you the other day, and I knew the fence was always open. Hell." He laughed. "Maybe it was me who broke the fence, I don't remember. Sometimes my memory fails. So I went down there, like I told you, to smoke a joint and chill and look up at the stars, man. You can get a whole new perspective on life when you do that. Lookin' up at infinity that way. So, when he come down with the chick, I recognized him, and I recognized the chick he had been talking to just the night before, tellin' her all about how his daddy was in the movies. In TV, CBS or NBC or some shit, man. He was gonna get her a job. An' he's workin' in a fuckin' bar, dude—but hey! He's just workin' his way through college because he is a really independent kind of guy!" He laughed. "And she is buyin' the whole thing. Women is fuckin' stupid sometimes, dude. No two ways about that.

"They come down the path, and I recognized him, and I recognized her, and I could not believe my eyes. I swear to God. I know I should have done something, man. I shouldn'a done what I did, I know that and I ain't proud of that. But, dude, I was stoned and the whole thing was just like, *surreal*, man. I'm lyin' there watchin' this thing goin' down and I'm like, dude, that is *Jimmy* there, man! And he is killin' that bitch! He was like crazy about that chick, and he's like, sitting on her and he's kissin' her like he's trying to fuckin' eat her, man!" He stared at me for a long time, then blinked, once, very slowly. "And, by the time I kind of came down—you know what I'm sayin'? and I'm thinkin' woah, you know, like what just happened?—she's already dead, and the cops are on the river with their lights, and he's runnin'."

I studied his face for a while, wondering what to ask him first. Finally I said, "Jimmy?"

He nodded slowly. "Yeah, man, Jimmy Fillmore. I won't never forget that name."

"So he ran or he didn't run, Wayne?"

He smiled and nodded. "I know, dude. We was negotiating, and I ain't gonna show all my hand, right? He ran. When him and the boat was gone, I put my leather on . . ."

I sighed and sat forward, with my elbows on the table. "You did what?"

"Oh, you know? It was a nice night, but that spot where I was layin'? It's got like stones and stuff, and them little prickly weeds. But I like it 'cause when the cops come down the river, they can't see you. That's why Jimmy had to run, right? So anyhow, I put on my leather and I went to have a look. And I'm thinkin' goddamn, man! He went and killed her! And I'm gonna call the cops. Truly, but then I thought, 'Wayne, don't be stupid, if you call the cops they are gonna pin this on you as sure as your name is Wayne

Harris.' So I thought I'd get me some insurance, and I collected up her shit and I buried it where I showed you."

"Insurance against what, Wayne?"

He laughed. "Are you kiddin' me? Have a look around, dude! I have one of those faces. Cops look at me and they say, 'That boy's guilty as *hell*! I don't know what he's done, but he is guilty of somethin'!' And here we are. Ain't it a good job I took out my insurance policy when I did?"

"Isn't it just. So where can I find this Jimmy Fillmore?"

He stared at me for a long moment from under hooded eyes. "You got a pen?"

I reached in my pocket and pulled out my pen. He lifted his wrists and showed me the manacles. I called in the guards and asked them to uncuff him. They released his hands and he took the pen from me, then studied the document. When they had gone, he said, "So what is your recommendation going to be, Stone?"

I thought it through, and finally I said, "Can you give me Jimmy's location?"

"If I can?"

I shrugged. I had no choice. I said, "If you can, the DA will give you your release."

He signed the papers and handed them back to me. I signed them too.

"He's workin' at a bar on Lafayette and Longfellow. It's a respectable café, you know what I'm sayin'? But the girls go in there for coffee and the dealers go in for a pie, from time to time. So if you're lookin' for somethin', well maybe you'll get lucky if you drop in at Eva Maria's Café." He pointed his finger at me like a gun again, only this time he wasn't manacled. "I'll tell you one thing for sure, Detective Stone, you get Jimmy's prints, you gonna find them on Angela's purse, maybe his DNA too. You should get a sample."

I gave him his copy of the deal and stood. "Thanks for the advice."

I called the guard, and as the door clanged open, Wayne said, "Hey, Stone."

I turned.

"What I told you is for real, man. I ain't a bad guy."

I turned and left.

FOURTEEN

Dehan was waiting for me when I got out. She had her ass on the trunk and her arms crossed over her chest. She had her hair tied up and her shades on and she looked beautiful and unhappy. She watched me approach and when I was a couple of feet away I handed her the file with the deal in it and showed her the laptop.

"You got your deal."

She gave a single nod. "It's not my deal, Stone. I couldn't get anything out of Teddy, except a promise he would get me the details today. Who did Wayne name?"

I went and opened the back of the car and put the laptop on the seat. "Jimmy Fillmore."

"Did he say where we could find him?"

"Of course, Eva Maria's Café on Lafayette and Longfellow."

"You still don't believe him."

I smiled at her. "Keys?" She tossed them to me. I caught them and said, "What I believe is irrelevant, Dehan."

I called the inspector. He answered on the first ring. "Stone. What news?"

"I have his testimony, sir. I think you and the DA should watch it."

"I have the assistant DA here with me now. Come right over, we'll watch it together. Did he give you a name?"

"Yes, sir. If what he says holds up, and I am pretty sure it will, we should have enough to arrest and convict Jimmy Fillmore. According to Harris, Fillmore's prints should be all over Angela Fernandez's purse, and, if he was responsible for the woman we found today, his prints and DNA should be on that body too. If the lab runs them, we'll know if he's in the system."

"I'll call Frank. You get here right away."

"Yes, sir."

We climbed in the car and as I started her up, Dehan said, "I'm sorry I got mad."

"I'm sorry I was a pain in the ass."

"You still are. Why did you send me to Teddy's bar?"

"To get Jimmy's details."

We pulled onto the bridge and started across the dark water. "Stone, enough already! Will you stop now, please?"

I glanced at her. After a moment I said, "I wanted to test a theory."

"And?"

I shrugged. "I don't know. We'll have to wait and see."

"Why won't you share your thoughts with me, Stone?"

"I already have, you don't agree. When you see the interview, you tell me what you think." I looked at her. "He is very convincing and he answered my doubts."

She made a face like "what the hell?" and spread her hands. "So you agree with me?"

I laughed. "Let's talk to Jimmy. For me, Dehan, there are still a few unanswered questions."

She sounded exasperated. "Like what? I'm your partner, Stone! Talk to me, for . . ."

She clenched her fists and made a couple of guttural noises, so I never got to know for whose sake. I sighed. "Okay!"

We crossed onto Randalls Island and I pretended to think. Finally I said, "For one thing, if Jimmy took the trouble to wear gloves and not leave prints with the latest girl this morning, how come he left his DNA in the form of semen?"

She frowned at me. "*What?*"

I looked at her like I was surprised. "How come . . . ?"

"No, I heard you. Frank has spoken to you? So soon?"

"No."

"Then how do you know he didn't leave prints and how do you know he left semen? For crying out loud, Stone!"

I smiled and raised my eyebrows high on my forehead. "You know my methods, Watson. You know the facts. Apply them, dear fellow."

What she answered was unrepeatable.

She watched me fixedly, with her arms crossed and her shades on top of her head, all the way back to the station. When I had parked and killed the engine, she said, "I know what you've done."

"You do?"

"You've cracked it. You've worked it out all on your own. I should hate you. I don't know why I don't."

"Because I am so lovable, Dehan. But." I raised a finger of caution. "Don't go jumping to conclusions. We are not home and dry yet, and I did not say that Jimmy was not involved. This is not a simple case."

She became serious. "Why'd you cut me out?"

"I didn't. I told you, but you wouldn't listen."

Her eyes went wide with exasperation again. "You told me about the stones and the prickly bushes, and about knowing where the stuff was. But you said he explained that!"

I nodded. "Exactly. Come on, Little Grasshopper, let's go see the movie."

Assistant DA Jason Malkovich was tall, lanky, and friendly. He had the word "seasoned" written into the lines on his face. He had prosecuted several of my arrests in the past and I knew he was a good man with a working brain in his head. I set up my laptop, the inspector closed the blinds, and we settled to watch the interview. We watched it in silence until the end, and when it had finished we sat in silence a little longer. Finally the inspector got up and opened the blinds.

He stood with his back to the window a moment, staring at the floor. Then he said, "John, I think some of your doubts were resolved here, in this interview."

Dehan looked at me, waiting to see what I said. I didn't say anything. The inspector looked at Malkovich. "Jason?"

He didn't look like he'd just won the lottery, but he nodded. "Obviously Harris' testimony on its own won't carry a lot of weight with a jury, but if the forensic evidence is there to corroborate it, we have a case. We need to pull in Fillmore and see what the lab can tell us about Angela's purse and the woman they found this morning."

I said, "I know Frank is pulling out all the stops . . ."

Malkovich smiled. "Pressure from on high is being brought to bear to prioritize this, John. We don't need the press running wild with a serial killer story."

Dehan raised an eyebrow. "Not to mention the fact that other girls might get killed."

He smiled at her without resentment. "We are all grown-ups here, Detective Dehan. We know what it means to the girls."

Her cheeks colored, but before she could answer I said, "I don't think there is much Detective Dehan or I can add to this discussion, sir. I think we would be better employed going to get Fillmore."

He nodded. "If anything comes up, I'll contact you."

Dehan stood, and as she did her phone rang. She looked at the screen, then at me. "Teddy." She swiped. "Yeah, Teddy, what have you got?" She took out her pad and leaned on the inspector's desk, taking a pen from his pot. "Yeah, yeah, it's okay, Teddy, I know you've been busy. Shoot." She recited as she wrote: "Top floor, seven fifty-seven Bryant Avenue. Thanks . . ." She paused. "What? His Social Security number? Yeah, give it to me." She scribbled it down, looked at the inspector, jerked her head at his laptop, and made typing motions with her fingers. He nodded and started rattling at the keyboard. She said into the phone: "Yuh. Yeah, don't worry about it. Better late than never. Bye."

She hung up and looked over the inspector's shoulder as he typed. After a moment she pointed and said, "Okay, that's him. James Philip Fillmore, Bryant Avenue, print it!" The inspector looked at her with raised eyebrows. She half grinned and said, "Sir?"

The printer spewed his photograph, general description, and last known address. I picked them up and looked at them. He fit the description we had from Wayne and Michael Shine. "Sir." I looked at the inspector. He and the assistant DA had got to their feet. "This address is two or three hundred yards from the café." I glanced at my watch. "At this time he is most likely to be at work. Dehan and I will go to the café. We need a car to go to his address and bring him in if he's there."

He nodded and reached for the phone. "Done. Get on it."

It was a ten-minute drive across the river on Bruckner Boulevard, then up Garrison and into Longfellow. I didn't figure we would need backup. In fact I was pretty sure, despite what I'd told the inspector, that he wasn't going to be there. Dehan didn't say anything to me during the drive, and I didn't feel much like talking either. I pulled up outside Eva Maria's Café and we went inside.

It was pretty much how Wayne had described it. Respectable and clean, at least on the surface, but the clientele was pretty representative of that area: people struggling to make ends meet, by whatever means available to them, and that meant anything from fifteen hours' hard work every day of the week to theft, prostitution, and violence. They were all there, drinking coffee, eating ham and eggs, and reading the paper at mock-pine, melamine tables, while Eva Maria turned a blind eye to anything that went down that she didn't need to see.

Suspicious faces pretended to ignore us. We ignored them

back and walked to the counter. Eva Maria, or whoever was in her shoes that day, gave us that "now what?" look. "Help you?"

I did something that could have been a smile if she'd wanted it to be, and asked her, "Jimmy in today?"

"Jimmy don't work here no more."

"Since when?"

"Since right now. He didn't show up this morning and now the cops are looking for him." She paused. "You *are* cops, right? You got the look."

I showed her my badge. "I got the badge too. Where is he?"

She shrugged and spread her hands. "Who am I? Yoda? There's a disturbance in the force on Bryant Avenue! Gimme a break! I told you, he didn't come in and he didn't call."

"You got an address for him?"

"What do I need an address for? He comes to me. I don't go to him. You want his Swiss bank account too? I got that back there along with his Social Security number. He's casual. I pay cash. End of story."

"You don't know where he lives?"

"I just got through tellin' you that."

Dehan slammed her open palm down on the counter and made a noise that seemed too big for such a delicate-looking hand. She snarled, "Can the attitude, Eva! We ain't vice, but I know a guy who is. You want we should start going through pockets here?"

There was an immediate scraping of chairs as people started getting to their feet and hurrying casually to the door. Eva spread her hands and looked past us at her departing customers. "Hey! What the . . . !"

"A little cooperation, Eva!"

"I don't know where he lives! What you want me to do? Get on my knees and pray for his address?"

Dehan leaned close to her and growled. "You got his phone number, Eva. Get it!"

She made a face that was a sullen scowl, looked in a notebook, and wrote down the number. She handed it to Dehan and said, "It's pay as you go. You won't get no address from it."

I nodded. "What about friends, girlfriends? He hook up with any of the girls?" She drew breath and her face told me she was going to lie. Before she could speak, I turned to Dehan. "Get Max, tell him what we've seen. Get him to put surveillance on this joint. Facilitating the traffic of prescribed substances . . ."

"Okay! Okay! Okay, already! She goes by the name Zena. Twenty maybe, Puerto Rican, she usually wears a little black leather skirt. She's got a stud in her nose and another in her belly button. She hangs out on the corner of Edgewater Road, by the railway tracks. She takes her tricks down to the park." She looked at the clock on the wall. "She should be there in an hour, maybe two. And for cryin' out loud, you didn't hear it from me!"

I smiled. "'Course not, Eva. We heard it from Yoda."

My cell started ringing as we stepped onto the street. Dehan sat on the hood of the Jag and watched me as I answered.

"John, it's John, here. The inspector." He clarified that in case I thought I was phoning myself. "Sergeant Solano is at Fillmore's last known address. The landlord says he hasn't been at that apartment for about two years. Has no idea where he is now."

"Okay, thank you, sir. Any word from the lab?"

"Pete Henson just called. He's sending in his preliminary results. He said Frank was about to call you about the girl."

I put it on speaker and sat next to Dehan. "Okay. What did Pete find?"

"He said there were prints on Angela's bag and you had asked him to compare them to Wayne Harris'. John, they were not a match."

Dehan looked into my face without expression. I said, "Did you tell him to compare them with Jimmy Fillmore's?"

"Yes, and he is doing that now."

"Good. What about the Jane Doe from this morning?"

"Frank is calling you about that now. Better you talk to him. Have you got Fillmore?"

I shook my head even though he couldn't see me. I had just heard the bleep of the call-waiting signal. "No, sir. He didn't come in today. We need to put out an APB on him. I have Frank waiting. I'll talk to you in a minute, sir."

I hung up and immediately it started ringing again. I put it on speaker for Dehan's benefit. "Frank. What have you got?"

"Let me just tell you these are results that would normally take weeks. You understand that. We are going flat out because of political pressure."

"Okay. What have you got?"

"The victim was Noelia Gomez, aka Cherry Pie, known to work Lafayette at Hunts Point. That's a little extra on the house, and you're welcome. A preliminary examination of the body, and please remember I have only had it a few hours, indicates bruising to the face, particularly around the mouth, consistent with having been punched or slapped. Bruising to the arms consistent with having been gripped tightly, but no prints, so he must have been wearing gloves."

"Size of his hands?"

"A large man as opposed to a small one, but impossible to be more precise than that, John."

"Okay, anything else?"

"Yes, of course, bruising from ligatures on the wrists and, as with Angela, extensive bruising and damage to the trachea from strangulation, most probably with the thumbs."

I glanced at Dehan. "What about semen and DNA?"

"There were traces of semen in her vagina and also on her skirt . . ."

"Whereabouts on her skirt?"

Dehan frowned at me and I could hear in his voice that Frank was frowning too. "On the hem, at the back, where you would expect it to be if it ran out."

"Okay, have you had time to run it?"

"Of course not. It takes time to get a profile, John. You know that. But we are working through the night. We might have something by tomorrow."

"Thanks, Frank. Stay in touch."

"Yeah, I don't stay in touch with my wife, but I should stay in touch with you."

He hung up and I looked at Dehan. Her eyebrows were high on her brow but her eyes were narrowed at me.

"You knew."

I nodded. "I told you."

"What does it mean?"

"It means that we get something to eat and then we go soliciting ladies of the night. Or in this case, ladies of the late afternoon."

"That's it. That's all you're going to tell me . . ."

I gave her a smile that was somewhere between smug and complacent. "You know my methods. You know the facts." I raised an eyebrow. "You and the inspector have underlined them to me often enough. You work it out."

I stood and went to open the car door. She watched me over her shoulder, muttered an obscene suggestion that was anatomically impossible, and got in the passenger side.

FIFTEEN

Zena looked as though she had achieved the anatomically impossible on at least one occasion and survived, at least physically, if not mentally, morally, and spiritually, to tell the tale—on a dedicated phone line and for a modest fee. Dehan was in the back seat pretending not to sulk, and I was cruising slowly up Edgewater Road trying to look seedy. I like to think that is not easy in a burgundy 1964 Jaguar Mark II. Zena was standing at the curb, watching me, chewing gum and looking both sulky and seedy in a black vinyl skirt. I slowed to a halt and leered at her. She gave me a chewing-gum smile back. "Hey, handsome, nice car. Lookin' for a party?"

"I am, and I think you're just the party I'm looking for."

She bent forward with her hands on her knees and gave a dirty little laugh. Then she caught sight of Dehan in the back and said, "Three-way is extra."

I tried to look like I cared. "How much?"

She glanced at the car, figured it was expensive, and said, "Hundred bucks?"

I grinned. "Call it two hundred and we'll throw in some coke and some French champagne. Hop aboard, sweet cheeks."

She giggled and ran coyly around the hood toward the

passenger side. I heard Dehan from the shadows behind me saying, "Sweet cheeks? Seriously?"

Zena climbed in and closed the door. I pulled away and she turned to smile at Dehan. "Hi," she said. "I'm Zena."

I smiled at the road ahead and said, "Hi, Zena, I am Detective Stone, and this is Detective Dehan. How are you doing today?"

She flopped back in her seat. "Motherfucker . . . !"

"Relax," I said. "We're not vice. We just want to talk to you about a friend of yours."

"Yeah, like that's gonna happen."

Dehan shifted her position so she could see Zena's face. "It's going to happen, Zena, because this guy is wanted for murder, and his latest victim was a sex worker, just like you. Now, we happen to know that you are one of his favorites, so if you are smart you'll tell us exactly what we need to know."

"One of my johns, killing hookers? You kidding me?"

I glanced in the mirror. "You see, Dehan? They are called hookers, not sex workers. Call me a dinosaur, but at least I have mastered the lingo."

She ignored me. "Not kidding, Zena. Raped and strangled last night."

She looked worried and a little sick. "Who's the john?"

"Jimmy, works at Eva Maria's Café."

She burst out in an ugly, cackling laugh. "*Jimmy?* Are you out of your *minds*?"

She looked at me like I was stupid. I offered her no expression back but asked her, "When was the last time you saw Noelia?"

She stopped grinning. "Noelia?"

"Yeah, you know, Cherry Pie. Seen her since last night?"

". . . no . . ."

Dehan cut in. "That would be because she was lying in the woods down at Ferry Point Park, dead, with Jimmy's semen inside her."

"Sweet Jesus . . ." She crossed herself and said a prayer under her breath. Then she looked over her shoulder at Dehan and said,

"She was with Jimmy last night. He come down to the corner after work and they went back to his place." She looked away. "Sweet mother . . . Jimmy . . . It's always the fuckin' sweet ones."

I said, "Where is Jimmy's place, Zena?"

She stared at me for a long moment before answering. Finally she said, "Second floor. Eleven twenty-one, Longwood, opposite the storage place."

I dropped her at the corner of Longfellow and Lafayette, turned west, and accelerated toward Garrison Avenue. I made the tires complain as I turned into Longwood and skidded to a halt outside an ugly, three-story redbrick with a small, blue plastic awning over the door. I got out and ran. Dehan was close behind me. As I rang on the bell and hammered on the door she said, "I called for backup," in a voice that said it was something I should have done.

I said, "Good," and hammered on the door again.

I pulled my Swiss Army knife from my pocket, selected the screwdriver, rammed it in the lock, gave it a firm whack with the butt of my automatic, and opened the door. Dehan stood staring at me. "Stone? What the hell are you doing? We haven't got a warrant or probable cause."

I yanked my knife out of the lock. "You haven't, Dehan, but I have. Coming? Or are you going to wait for backup?"

There was a steep, narrow staircase with wooden steps showing through a frayed carpet that was of no recognizable color. I sprinted up, with my Smith & Wesson still in my hand. There was only one door on that floor. I hammered on it and shouted, "Jimmy Fillmore, NYPD, open up!"

I heard Dehan's feet on the stairs behind me. She had her weapon in her hand and went to stand on the far side of the doorway. She frowned and shook her head, whispering, "*Stone, we can't do this!*"

I ignored her, listening for sounds inside. There were none. I gave the door a once-over. It looked flimsy. I stood back and put all my two hundred and twenty pounds behind a hefty kick at the lock. The wood splintered and a second kick burst the door open. I didn't look at Dehan, but I was pretty sure she was as distressed as the door.

I went in with my gun held out in front of me, shouting, "*NYPD! Show yourself!*"

It was a small, shabby room with two sash windows overlooking Longwood Avenue. On the left there was a door that led into a small kitchen, and between the two windows a small dining table with two chairs. To the right of the door there was a sofa and a coffee table in front of an old TV. The TV was sitting on a wooden crate up against the wall.

Jimmy was sitting on the sofa, with his right elbow resting on the arm. He was gaping at the TV, which was odd because the TV was turned off. I ignored him and moved to a door opposite the kitchen. It gave onto a bedroom. The drapes were drawn and the room was dark, and smelled of cigarettes and stale sweat. There was an aluminum-frame bed with the covers thrown back, showing old, stained sheets. Another door stood open onto a bathroom. I checked in there but it was empty, so I went back to Jimmy.

He was still gaping, but now I could see clearly his eyes were rolled back in their sockets, and the left side of his head had a neat hole plugged into the temple. I walked around and saw that most of the right side of his head was missing, and the sofa and the wall were spattered with blood and gore. It looked as though it was still wet. In his left hand he was holding a 9mm Taurus semiautomatic. Dehan was staring at him. I crouched down to sniff the gun. It had been fired recently. Dehan frowned at me.

"This isn't funny anymore, Stone."

"It never was."

"How did you know?"

I felt a small twist of irritation in my gut but suppressed it. I stood and said, "I didn't know, Dehan, but it was a possibility. A probability, given the facts."

She narrowed her eyes and shook her head. "How? Why?

How was this a probability? How could you possibly guess that he might commit suicide?"

I sighed, but before I could answer we heard the sirens of two patrol cars approaching. I shook my head. "I can't go through the whole explanation now, Dehan. It was there to be figured out if you'd had an open mind. You want to call it in? I want to have a look around before the crime scene team kick us out." Her eyes were bright with anger. I added, "Please don't get mad. I will explain it, just not right now."

She yanked her phone from her pocket and walked to the window. I stood back by the bedroom door and examined the scene. From where I was I could see into the kitchen. I went in and looked around. I could hear Dehan talking behind me. On the draining rack by the sink I saw a small breakfast bowl, a mug, a cereal spoon, and a teaspoon. There was also a knife and a fork and two glasses. I stepped over and had a closer look at the glasses. They still had droplets of water in them. I had a look in the trash and in the recycling bin. There was no bottle. I smiled, took my cell, and took several photographs of the scene. Then I took two evidence bags from my pocket and carefully placed one glass in each.

"What are you doing?"

I turned to face Dehan. I could hear feet tramping up the stairs. I pointed at the glasses. "What did they drink?"

I moved out of the kitchen to meet the uniforms coming up the stairs. I showed them my badge. "Crime scene and the ME are on their way. Get some tape up for me, would you? And see who's upstairs and if they heard anything."

I knew they'd get squat, but you have to try. One of them went downstairs to get the tape and the other made his way up to the next floor, taking his pad from his pocket. Dehan was in the kitchen doorway. She seemed to be mad, and also a bit upset. She spoke without looking at me. "So there was somebody here and they had a drink."

"It looks that way."

"But whoever was here took whatever they were drinking away with them."

I nodded. "That's what it looks like."

"And that is significant, why?"

I shrugged. "Maybe it isn't."

She sighed noisily, put on her latex gloves, and went into the bedroom. I heard her open the wardrobe and went to watch. There was nothing in there save a few old clothes. She closed it and got on all fours to peer under the bed. Again there was nothing of interest there, only a pair of shoes and a lot of dust. Finally she came to the chest of drawers beside the bed. She went through it methodically and found what I had guessed she was looking for in the bottom drawer, under a spare set of sheets. It was a shoebox. She took a photograph of it in the drawer, then removed it, set it on the bed, and opened it. Then she photographed it again.

The first thing she took out was a pair of torn, pink panties that appeared to be stained. She put them in an evidence bag and set it to one side. I stepped over beside her and looked down. The box contained a small hairbrush with a few dark hairs in it, several silk handkerchiefs, and several photographs. One was of Angela, one of Cherry Pie, the others were of similar girls whom I did not recognize. Most of them, but not all, were dressed like Cherry; all were smiling for the camera, and Jimmy was in a couple of them.

I hunkered down beside her as Dehan went through them one by one. They seemed to be in a bar, and Jimmy was raising his glass to the camera, with his left arm around one girl or another. Dehan said, "Are these the ones that got away? Or are they lying in the morgue, waiting for somebody to give them a name?"

She bagged everything, including the box, and left it back in the drawer.

We heard the heavy tramping of feet and after a moment a voice called my name from the next room. I went out and saw Frank and Pete Henson at the door with their assistants. They ducked under the tape and I pointed at Jimmy on the sofa.

"He's all yours, Frank. Cause of death seems pretty self-evident, but I'd be curious to know what his last meal consisted of."

He paused on his way to the body and frowned at me. "Really?"

I nodded. "Really."

"I wouldn't normally do an autopsy on somebody who had shot himself in the head. It's what we call in the profession a damn waste of time."

"Will you make an exception in this case, please, Frank?"

He shrugged. "Fine."

I showed Pete the glasses and asked him to go over the whole kitchen. Then Dehan took him to the bedroom and showed him the box. After that, he and Frank asked us to go away and let them do their jobs.

We walked down the stairs in silence and carried that same silence through the gathering dusk back to the station. There we climbed the stairs in silence and didn't break it until we knocked on the inspector's door.

"Come!"

Dehan opened the door and we went in.

"Ah! The dynamic duo!" He gestured with both hands at the two seats opposite him. "Please, sit. What progress?"

I turned to Dehan. "You want to explain, Dehan? I think this is more your success than mine."

She raised an eyebrow at me and the inspector beamed. "Success? So you have Jimmy Fillmore?"

Dehan took a deep breath. "It looks that way, sir. It also looked as though he decided to spare the city the cost of a trial. Frank will have to confirm it, but it looks as though he shot himself in the head while sitting on the sofa. In his bedroom we found a box full of what appear to be trophies from his kills, though obviously, again, the lab will have to confirm that. It contained panties that probably belonged to Noelia Gomez, his last victim, and to Angela Fernandez. There was also a ladies' hairbrush, containing long, dark hairs, that should give us enough material to identify the owner, and photographs of Noelia, Angela, and several other girls. Jimmy is with them in a couple of the pictures."

The inspector listened carefully throughout, and when she had finished he smiled broadly. "Excellent work. Then we can consider, pending the lab results, that this case is closed."

"It would certainly look that way, sir."

He turned to me. "John, I know you had your doubts, but I trust this has satisfied even your relentlessly incisive mind. And I have to say, all credit to you, John, you never let your own, personal feelings interfere with the investigation. You are a true example to us all, and I might say a superb role model for Carmen. Commendable work, both of you. I think you have earned a couple of days off, don't you?"

I smiled. "Thank you, sir."

We left and made our way down the stairs again. We collected our things and stepped out into the gathering evening. When we got to the car Dehan stopped and put her hand on my chest. There was a wash of amber light on her face from the streetlamp above her.

"Okay, John, let's stop this before it gets out of hand. Tell me what the hell is going on in your mind. Don't bullshit me and don't fob me off. What the hell do you know that you are not telling me?"

I raised my eyebrows high. "John?"

"I warn you that I am getting mad. Don't push me any further. Tell me or I am going to lose it."

I nodded. "Okay, let's go and grab a meal somewhere and I will tell you what is on my mind. No need to get mad."

"Emilio's Pizza and we walk home. And quit bullshitting me!"

"Deal."

SIXTEEN

WE ORDERED STEAK AND FRIES AND A BOTTLE OF WINE, and while he cooked them, we drank a couple of beers. We took a while, sipping and looking at each other, to find our way back across the bridges we were building in silence while we drank. Eventually I smiled at her and she smiled back. It was a nice smile, which she followed up with, "You know you are one obstinate son of a bitch, don't you?"

I nodded. "My mother, God rest her soul, used to tell me the same thing, in those very same words."

She lifted her thumb, not as a "thumbs-up" but as a "number one," and said, "One: How did you know, quote, 'that something bad was going to happen'?" She lifted her index finger. "Two: How did you know there would be fingerprints on Angela's bag and not on Noelia's body, and that there would be semen?" She lifted her middle finger. "How did you know, or suspect, that something had happened to Jimmy Fillmore? And why is it significant that somebody took away the bottle after they had had a drink together?"

I pulled off half my beer and wiped my mouth on the back of my hand. "Those 'why' questions will get you into trouble, Dehan. They are too vague. They don't focus your mind."

"Keep doing that. Keep bullshitting me. I swear you will sleep on the couch."

"I'm not. And you'll have to wrestle me for the bed and you know how that always ends up."

"Quit stalling."

"I had a hunch something bad was going to happen because, if Wayne wasn't our killer, then our killer had to be out on the street, and still active. So it stood to reason that he might kill again at any time . . ."

She cut across me, shaking her head. "But at that time you believed that Wayne *was* the killer."

I raised a finger. "It works that way too, if you think about it. And in any case, I believed he *might* be the killer because I was not happy with some of the details of his story."

She frowned like she was getting a headache.

"*What . . . ?*"

I ignored her and went on. "The fingerprints on the purse, Dehan, you really should be able to answer for yourself . . ."

She groaned softly, then raised a hand and said, "Okay, okay, give me a second." She thought and I waited. Finally she said, "He met her in a social environment, like a bar or something. They had arranged to meet to have a drink or whatever. In that kind of setting he could not be wearing gloves, so there was a good chance he handled her purse when he subdued her, bound her, and gagged her. He wouldn't have had time to put on gloves, but anyway he wouldn't care because he planned to remove the purse anyway. But with Noelia, by the time he strangled and murdered her, he had already put on his gloves."

I smiled and made a noncommittal face. "Sounds reasonable."

"But how could you have known there would be semen?"

I stared at her for a long moment. "You really don't see it?"

"No!"

"He always dumps them in the river."

"And the river washes away the traces of semen and DNA."

I half shrugged. "In the cold weather the bodies sink. By late

April or May the water warms up. There are a lot of bacteria in the water and they very quickly corrupt any DNA such as semen that might be in the body."

"But . . ."

I raised my eyebrows and began to nod slowly as she narrowed her eyes. Before she could say anything, a reporter on the TV spoke a name that made us turn toward the bar.

". . . Wayne Harris was released from prison this afternoon having served only six months of a five-year sentence for possession of cocaine. That in itself may not be very remarkable, but what is remarkable is the reason for his release. It seems that he has assisted the police in the capture of a serial killer who had been active in the Bronx area for at least two years—possibly much longer than that—while the police were completely oblivious to his murderous activity. It was not until Wayne Harris alerted them to his killings that they became aware. Since then, the police have uncovered a total of four murders committed by the man some are referring to as the Westchester Creek Strangler . . ."

Emilio brought over our steaks and set them in front of us. Then he poured our wine, nodding while he did it. He set down the bottle and gestured at me with the back of his hand while making his right leg do a little dance. "Eh," he said. "You're a cop, right?"

I nodded. "Yeah, so is my partner."

He turned to Dehan. "Yeah, you're a cop too. This guy. He killed however many young women. Now, they gonna use my money to keep him in jail. Why'd they get rid of the chair? Answer me that!"

I shook my head. "I don't know, Emilio. But this guy ain't going nowhere on your dollar. He's dead. Listen to the rest of the news item."

He nodded, watching me. "Oh, he's dead?"

"Yeah."

"Good. Death is too good for him, but I'm glad. Enjoy your meal."

The TV was saying, ". . . in a bizarre twist to this tale, detectives found Fillmore dead in his apartment this afternoon, having apparently shot himself in the head . . ."

Emilio called over, "Hey, yeah, you was right! Nice."

I gave him the thumbs-up and turned back to Dehan.

She cut into her steak. Her expression was serious. "How did you know?"

"That he was dead?"

"Yeah."

I chewed for a while, then sipped the wine. Eventually I said, "I didn't." She scowled at me. "I didn't know, Dehan. He didn't go into work. He didn't call. From what I had heard from Teddy, he was reliable, so that was odd. And . . ." I sighed deep and shrugged. "Don't get mad, but in my reasoning, one of the possibilities was that Jimmy was being framed, and if he was, the real killer had to eliminate him before we caught him."

She put her head in her hands. "But, Stone, you said at the beginning that you knew something was going to happen because . . ."

"It gets confusing for me too, sometimes, Dehan. But the big difference between me and most other investigators is that, instead of making up my mind at the beginning, I keep all the options open, and then make up my mind when I have actual proof."

"Do you know how smug you sound when you say that?"

"Yes."

"Well this time, Mister Smug Ass, you were wrong, and I was right. Jimmy Fillmore was guilty."

"And Wayne Harris is a free man."

She gave her head a little tilt to the side. "A fair price, I think."

"Perhaps."

"Come on, Stone!" She laughed. "Admit this once that you were wrong. Have you ever been wrong? Ever? Just once?"

"No."

"*Never? Seriously?*"

"Never. How can you be wrong if you never make up your

mind until you have proof? But before we move on from this subject, let me leave you with a thought. What was missing from Angela's purse?" She frowned, shook her head. I said, "Lipstick."

She stared at me for a long moment. "That's it. You are so sleeping on the couch tonight."

"You'll have to wrestle me for the bed."

"It's on, boy." She pointed at me. "You are going *down!*"

I raised an eyebrow at her. "Something to look forward to."

Her eyes went wide, her jaw dropped, and she started to laugh.

We finished our meal, and the wine, laughing. Emilio had some goat's cheese he claimed he'd had brought in in the Italian ambassador's diplomatic bag—a statement he accompanied with an elaborate wink. The Italian ambassador, he said, was his cousin Tony, and he laughed raucously. The cheese was good, but the wine was gone before the cheese was, so I had a Bushmills and Dehan had a brandy, and somehow it was eleven by the time we stepped out and started strolling home, arm in arm and still laughing.

We'd walked maybe a hundred yards. We were almost at the corner of Haight Avenue when my phone rang. We looked at each other and sighed. I didn't recognize the number. I answered, "Yeah, Stone, who is this?"

"Good evening, Detective Stone Cold. How are you feeling? Are you feeling triumphant tonight?"

"What do you want, Wayne? It's eleven o'clock at night."

"I'm aware of the time, John. I am just here celebrating and I wanted to thank you for your help in securing my freedom."

"No thanks required. Please don't call this number again."

"Well, now, Detective Stone, here's the thing. I think that you and I need to talk."

"We've done our talking, Wayne. We're done here."

"Not so fast, Detective Stone Cold, not so fast. See, there are some details that we have not covered, and you are going to want to cover them, I promise you."

I glanced at Dehan and puffed my cheeks. "Yeah? Then come into the station tomorrow morning. We'll talk there."

He laughed out loud. "Oh man! Like a big shot executive, contact my office! Dude! You cannot treat me like that. I need your respect, man."

"Goodbye, Wayne."

"Tonight."

"*What?*"

Dehan was watching me through narrowed eyes. I spread my hands at her and shook my head. I said into the phone, "You want to meet *tonight*? Get real, Wayne!"

His voice changed. "No. It's time you got real, Detective Stone. You've known from the start that there was more to this than met the eye. Well, my friend, you were right. You get yourself down to Randall and Zerega and I'll be waiting for you. You're gonna want to hear what I have to tell you. And Stone? Come alone, pal. If I see your cute partner with you, or I smell bacon on the air, I am out of there. *Comprende?*"

The line went dead. I stared at Dehan for a moment. "Come on, I'm driving you home. I have to go to Zerega Avenue."

I took her arm and started to walk back toward the car, outside Emilio's. She said, "I'm coming with you. You are not going alone."

"A, if he sees you he'll bolt. B, I am not letting you within a mile of that man."

"What does he want?"

"He says he wants to tell me what the case was all about."

She frowned. "What does that mean?"

We had got to the car and I opened the door. "You and your open questions, Dehan. One day they will get you into trouble. I'm serious. Get in."

We got in and slammed the doors. I fired up the engine and took off toward Haight Avenue again. I said, "It means that Wayne never knew we had Rosario and Sonia. Tonight he was watching the news and he found out."

She shook her head as I accelerated toward our house. "So? Stop talking in riddles, Stone!"

I skidded to a halt outside our front door and climbed out. I had my piece in my hand. "I haven't got time now, Dehan."

She pulled her weapon and I opened the door. I flipped on the light and we checked every room. There was nobody there. I ran down the stairs to the living room and at the front door I held her by her shoulders. "Listen, expect a call from me in about half an hour. Don't talk, just listen and record the call. If necessary, call for backup. I'll be where Angela was murdered."

"Jesus, Stone . . ."

"The answer to your questions is lipstick!"

I ran down the steps, climbed back in the Jag, did a U, and accelerated south, toward Zerega and the Westchester Creek.

Sinatra called New York the city that never sleeps. That may be true of Manhattan, but the vast residential and industrial areas in the Bronx, Brooklyn, Queens, and the rest—after sundown, they become empty, dark places, with shadows that are only made deeper by the lifeless streetlamps that bathe the blacktop and the sidewalks in dead orange and amber. You don't see anybody in those desolate streets, except the occasional lost soul: lost not because they don't know the way home, but because they have no home to find their way to.

I drove fast through these spiritual wastelands, and eventually passed under the multiple bridges of the Bruckner and Cross Bronx expressways, like huge portals into the underworld. There I joined the path of the Westchester Creek that ran black and cold beside me on the left, and soon came to Randall Avenue on my right.

All the parking spaces, packed full during the day, were empty now. But up ahead, on the left, I saw the dark silhouette of a BMW. I slowed and pulled in a couple of spaces away, just past the gate where we had recently gained access to the river. I killed the engine, dialed Dehan's number, put the phone back in my pocket, and climbed out. Ten yards away, in a pool of sickly light from a streetlamp, I saw a figure climb out of the BMW and close the door. He lit up a cigarette and by the flame of his lighter I saw it was Wayne.

He took a deep drag and put his lighter away, then walked toward me, blowing smoke. His footsteps were loud in the stillness of the night. Finally he stood in front of me, massive, menacing, and smiling. "Hello, Detective Stone Cold. This is the first time I have seen you when you haven't had my future in your hands. It feels good."

"What do you want, Wayne?"

He laughed. "That question again. It's what my therapist kept asking me inside: 'What do you want, Wayne?'" He shrugged and chuckled. "It's a stupid question. What you want changes from one moment to the next, don't it, Stone? Half an hour ago you wanted to cuddle up in bed with your cute lady. Now, just thirty minutes later, you want to find out what I know. And in another thirty minutes, who knows what you'll want then?"

"I'm getting bored. Have you got something for me or not?"

"Oh, I have got something for you, Stone, for sure." He shook his head. "Ask not what a man wants, John, ask always what a man intends. What he wants may change from one moment to the next, but if he is a man, what he intends will remain constant."

"All right, Wayne, what do you intend?"

"I thought I had made that clear, John."

"Cut to the chase. You've got thirty seconds. Then I am getting in my car and I am going home. Your bullshit bores me, Wayne. Get to the point."

He stared at me for a long moment and his eyes were dangerous. There was a hunger in them, and a suppressed rage. "Thirty seconds? Is that all you give me? Thirty seconds and counting. What are we down to now? Twenty? Fifteen?"

I sighed, pulled my keys from my pocket, and turned toward my car.

He spoke from behind me: "Always with the ultimatums. Or

should that be ultimata?" I opened the door and went to climb in. He said, "I want—I *intend*—to tell you the truth."

SEVENTEEN

I PAUSED, LOOKING AT HIM ACROSS THE ROOF OF MY car. I spoke with more anger than I had intended. "Is this going to be fifteen hours of B-movie bad guy bullshit? Or do you *intend* to get to the point before breakfast? Because I am telling you I am not interested in being a captive audience of the Wayne Harris Show. You are not amusing and you are not interesting. So unless you have something to tell me, Wayne, you can go to hell!"

He studied the tip of his cigarette. "I think you will be interested in what I have to tell you."

"So tell me."

He smiled and pointed down toward the river. "Down there."

"Are you kidding? You want to go down to the river?"

He nodded. "I need to show you something."

I pulled my 1911, pointed it at him, and cocked the hammer. "Okay, show me something."

His face went tight. "You pulled a gun on me? Man, you are so uptight."

"Lean on the car." He put the butt in his mouth and leaned on the car. I patted him down. He was clean. "Okay, walk. Show me."

He pushed himself off the car and moved toward the gate in

the fence. We went through and he began to stumble and slide down the track toward the river. A waxing moon in its first quarter was rising, ghostly and orange, over Brooklyn, but offered no light on the path, which was dense with shadows.

Finally he broke out onto the flatter ground and ran a couple of steps. I followed after him and he stopped and turned to face me. He looked at my weapon and shook his head. "Put your gun away, Detective. I don't know what to do to make you trust me, man."

I looked around, listening. "Telling the truth might be a start," I said. "Sit down."

He nodded. "That's what I brought you here for. To tell you the whole truth." He sat and I started to inspect the undergrowth surrounding us while he continued to speak. "You're a smart man, Stone. A lot of cops are stupid. You know that? But you—you're smart. What I told you was the truth, but it wasn't all the truth, and you saw that."

When I was satisfied we were alone, I returned to where he was sitting, found a rock, and sat where I could see the path up to the road. I released the hammer and holstered my gun.

"You saw the news, huh?"

He chuckled. "Yeah, I saw the news. I'm a hero!"

"You didn't know we'd found Rosario and Sonia."

He shook his head and waved his hands in circles. "But, dude, you jump to so many conclusions on the basis of nothin'. I told you there were other girls. I told you he was talkin' to some chicks. The only one I *witnessed* was Angela."

I smiled without much humor. "So what am I doing here?"

He wagged a finger at me like I had been naughty. With his left hand he took a last drag on his cigarette, dropped it on the turf, and crushed it out with his toe. "I knew! I knew that you would start overthinking things, and read too much into these other chicks. And I thought, if we could have a private conversation, just you and me, we could resolve any doubts that you have." He leered. "You feel me?"

I shrugged. "The DA believes you, my inspector believes you, why do you care what I think?"

He nodded down at his feet. "Because you, my friend, are a Rottweiler. You grab a hold of somethin' and you will not let go. Even if you're wrong. I know dudes like you, and I am never gonna get a day's rest as long as I have you on my tail."

"So what are you going to show me, Wayne? Jimmy's trophies from Rosario and Sonia?"

He sat upright and spread his hands. "Now, how in the world would I know where to find them?"

"You tell me, Wayne. The same way you got hold of Angela's and Cherry's panties. The same way you got hold of all those photographs."

"I don't know what you're talkin' about, Stone. I think you have developed a fixation." He leaned forward, with his elbows on his knees, and pointed at me. "You know what I think? I think you are sufferin' from a bad case of jealousy."

I smiled. "Really?"

"Your cute Detective Dehan, man, she could put the cuffs on me any day. You think I ain't noticed the way she looks at me?" He grinned. "All that anger and hostility, man, that masks passion and hunger. A woman like that, with all that animal power, she is drawn to a badass like me. It ain't cerebral, Stone . . ." He shook his head. "Her relationship with you? That's love. I can see that. It's a connection of two minds. But with me? Dude, it is pure animal biology. That pony wants this cowboy to ride her."

There was a hot rage in my belly, but I was not going to let him see it. Not yet. Instead I kept the smile fixed, shook my head, and gave a small laugh. "You're sloppy, Wayne. You overrate your own intelligence. An IQ of 145? What did you do, get a DIY Home IQ Test? You sure it wasn't just 45? Let me tell you what happened. You called Jimmy and you told him not to go to work, because you were going to go and visit him. As soon as you got out you went straight to his apartment. You took a bottle of rum with you, to celebrate your release. You sat with him on the sofa and filled his head with all that pretentious shit you talk, and then you shot him. You wiped your prints off the gun and squeezed his hand onto the butt and the trigger. Then you took the glasses to the kitchen, washed the prints off them, and left, taking your bottle of rum with you, because you remembered you had told me you liked rum."

"That's quite a story."

"It's more than a story, Wayne."

"Yeah?" He laughed. "How you gonna prove it? You ain't got no witness."

"Witness? Oh, I have a witness, Wayne. I have you. You are at least intelligent enough to know that a guilty plea can seriously affect sentencing. You will plead guilty."

He laughed out loud. "You are one crazy son of a bitch, Stone. How'd you figure that?"

"Well, for a start, there is the circumstantial evidence."

"Yeah? Like what?"

"Like the fact that Jimmy did not own a gun, and he was too timid and mild ever to have fired a gun. He was all talk, he was a fantasist, but there was no way on Earth that he was violent. He did not belong to a gun club and he did not own a gun."

"That is bullshit and you know it. New York is full of dudes who own guns that are not registered."

"Second, and a little more persuasive, is the fact that, in those photographs you helpfully left in the box, you can see clearly that Jimmy was right-handed. We can find a hundred witnesses to testify to that if we need to." I studied his face. He was expressionless. Somewhere on the river a barge moaned. The orange moon was turning silver and her molten light warped on the black water. I shrugged. "I guess it must have been awkward. That was his spot on the sofa. That was where he always sat, with his right elbow on the arm. You couldn't very well say to him, 'Hey, Jimmy, you mind if I sit there and you sit here? Only, I have to shoot you in the right temple.' So you banked, correctly as it happens, on the authorities' willingness to turn a blind eye to small details, so long as they could report to the press that the Westchester Creek Strangler was no longer a threat."

He grunted. "That is . . . odd. You might get some people scratchin' their heads. But it ain't conclusive, not by a long chalk."

I shrugged. "Maybe. You know? It is really hard to shoot yourself in the temple, even with your dominant hand. There are all those autonomic responses that make your hand waver at the last minute, plus the recoil. Most people who try it wind up maiming themselves instead. To manage such a lethal shot with his left hand, that is almost impossible. But, you are right, it is not conclusive. To be conclusive I would need something that showed that you had definitely been at the apartment shortly before his body was found."

He shook his head. "There ain't no way in hell you ever going to prove that."

I stared at him for a long moment. "You're stupid, Wayne. And you know what makes you stupid? Your vanity and, above all, your laziness. You spend so much time thinking about how damn smart you are, you forget to actually *be* smart. Being smart, Wayne, is something you *do*, not something you *are*."

"What are you talkin' about?"

"Being smart means *thinking*. And thinking means learning, studying, *knowing* your subject. Not memorizing smart quotes that make you look and sound smart."

"Cut to the chase, Stone."

I laughed. "Dude, chill, man, you have such a bad attitude." I sat a moment, smiling at him, enjoying his discomfort. Eventually I said, "The glasses, Wayne. You should have dried them and put them away. For a start, why would he have two glasses there when everything else on the rack was a single item? One plate, one knife, one fork, but two glasses. On its own, that means almost nothing, but added to the left-hand shot? It tells us there was somebody else in the apartment. The glasses were still wet, so they were used very recently, and whoever used them took the bottle away with them. What would make them do that? Well, the fact that they didn't want me to know they drank rum. Careless and sloppy, Wayne. Very careless and very sloppy. But the most important thing? The really, really stupid thing?"

His face was as tight as a bowstring. He said, "Stop calling me stupid, Stone."

I leaned forward. "What was really *stupid*, Wayne, was that after you washed off your fingerprints, you rinsed the glass under the tap and put the glasses on the rack. Leaving fresh prints."

"They were wet. You can't leave prints on a wet surface."

"I don't know where you got that gem, Wayne, but it's bullshit, just like everything else in your head. Those prints are being processed right now. And you are going down for Jimmy's murder, as well as Angela's and all the others. You are not a genius, Wayne, you're a moron."

I was expecting it, but even so, his size, his weight, his strength, and the sheer rage of his attack overwhelmed me. I am not small, but he was a giant. He collided with me and threw me on my back. He straddled me, sitting on my belly. His massive hands fastened around my throat, he locked his elbows, and his thumbs began to press into my windpipe. His face was twisted and contorted with rage and hatred.

My instinctive reaction was to grip at his wrists and his arms, but I knew that if I did that I would never have the strength to pull him off. I would be signing my own death warrant. My lungs were screaming for air and my heart was pounding in my ears. I groped for a rock, anything solid, but there was nothing there. I was going, slipping into darkness.

Then, it may have been panic, I don't know, but a furious rage welled up inside me and I twisted and rammed my forearm savagely into his locked elbow, forcing the joint the wrong way. He didn't let go, but he howled with pain and his grip slipped. I rammed again, twice, and he stood, backing away, holding his arm, swearing. I was still suffocating, but I knew I could not give him time to recover. I scrambled and charged him, roaring like something demented, with a mixture of rage, fear, and sheer relief at getting air into my lungs. I smashed my head into his chest. He went over backward and I stumbled, tripped, and fell sprawling just beyond him, rolling down the slope into cold, shallow water.

I staggered to my feet and started to scramble up the slope, gulping air as I went. I got to the top with my legs shaking. He was standing just eight or ten feet away. His left arm was hanging limp by his side. I said, "Give it up, Wayne. It's over."

As I said it I reached for my weapon. He moved with the speed of a viper. He leapt at me, swinging his right fist. I leaned back but not far enough and the rock in his hand caught me a glancing blow on my temple. The pain was like a knitting needle being driven through my skull. I staggered back and he lashed out with his foot, catching me on the thigh. I fell painfully and rolled down the slope again, into the shallow pools of water. Sharp stones stabbed into my back and for a moment I went into spasm, unable to move or breathe. Above me I could see his silhouette, standing at the top of the slope, with the rock still in his hand.

He half ran, half skidded down and stood over me. Thin shards of pain shot through my lungs. Air rasped in my throat. I wondered if I had broken my back. I could feel the water lapping at the side of my cheeks and my mouth, and I knew what he was going to do. He was going to beat me unconscious with the rock and then drown me, facedown in the black river. I thought of Dehan and knew I could not let that happen. He knelt and loomed over me, leering down into my face.

"First you," he said. "Then I'm going to pay a visit to your cute Detective Dehan. I'm gonna ride me that pony tonight."

I struggled to focus. I moved first my toes and then my fingers, and knew my back was not broken. Wayne raised the rock in his right hand, high above his head. I had maybe a second, at most. It was enough. His vanity would betray him.

I said, "Wait, if you're going to kill me, at least tell me first. Was it you who killed Angela? Was it you?"

He threw back his head and laughed. Then he grinned down

at me. "Yeah, I did. I killed 'em all, right here. This is my killin' hill on the River Styx. And wouldn't you love to know how!"

I said, "You're under arrest, Wayne."

He snorted. "Fuck you. Now you gonna be real Stone Cold."

He raised the rock again, gritted his teeth. I pulled the 1911 from my holster and shot him through the heart. He looked very surprised, then slowly keeled over and fell into the dark waters where he had cast the bodies of all the young girls he'd killed.

All but one.

EIGHTEEN

I DRAGGED MYSELF UP ONTO THE BANK AND LAY gasping for thirty long seconds. Then I reached into my jacket and pulled out my phone, saying, "Dehan! Did you get that? Did you call for backup . . . ?"

I stared at the screen. I was not connected. My brain ached. I called Dispatch. "This is Detective Stone requesting backup at Randall and Zerega. Notify the inspector. Wayne Harris is dead. I'll need a team and the ME."

I hung up and struggled to the top of the bank, trying to think. I called Dehan.

"The number you are calling is turned off or out of range. Please try again later . . ."

A burning pellet of dread seared in my belly. I ran, scrambling, stumbling and falling through the dark, up the track toward the gate in the fence. I burst out onto the road, gasping, my heart pounding in my ears, trying to think, trying to make sense of what was happening. Somewhere in the night sirens were wailing. Two patrol cars skidded around the corner from Randall Avenue. I hailed them and they screeched to a halt in front of me. As they climbed out I shouted at the nearest, "Secure the scene! Wayne Harris is down there. He's dead. You!" I turned to the other. "Get on to Dispatch. Have a car go to my house, *now*! Detective Stone's house! Haight Avenue! Check on Detective Dehan! See if she is there! Now! *Do it now!*"

She was already talking on the radio. I was running for my car. My phone was ringing. I fumbled for it, praying it would be Dehan. It was the inspector. I answered as I clambered into the Jag.

"Stone! What the *hell* is this? Harris is *dead*?"

I said, "I haven't got time. I think Dehan may be too. Get off the line."

"*What?* Stone! Talk to me! *Where?*"

Where?

I said, "I don't know." My mind was reeling. "I left her at home. There's a car going there now."

"You left her at home? John, you're not making sense. Where are you? Are you at the river?"

I was at the river. I was at the river where all the killings had gone down.

All but one.

"Yes. I'm at the river."

"What the hell are you doing there?"

"He called me."

"Who did? Wayne Harris?"

My mind was beginning to clear. "Yes. He called me and told me he wanted to talk to me, alone. He said he didn't want to see Dehan there. He said he wanted to tell me the truth."

"What truth?"

"That he had killed the girls."

"That doesn't make any sense, John!"

"No, it doesn't . . ."

"John, are you sure of all this . . . ?"

Was I sure? I stared out of the windshield at the black mass of the trees and struggled to put the pieces together. But something was wrong. Something didn't fit. In the distance I could hear more sirens wailing across the Bronx. I heard the crackle of a radio. Then there was a uniform running toward me. The inspector's voice in my ear: "John! John, are you there?"

"Sir?" The patrolman's face was at the door of my car, peering at me. "Sir, the lights are on at your house, but nobody is answering."

Wild panic was pounding in my chest. I shouted, *"Blow out the lock! Smash the window! Get in there! Get in there now!"*

I slammed the door. Fired up the engine, spun the wheel, and went screaming north up Zerega. A voice in my head kept screaming at me that somehow he had got to Dehan. Somehow he had got to her. But how? *That* was the truth he had wanted to tell me. The one shred of hope I clung to was that her body had not been there. All his other victims had on that spot, by the river. That was where he killed.

All but one.

Then everything went into slow motion. Up ahead on the left I saw Teddy's Late-Night Bar. It was closed. I heard a horrible noise in my head and realized it was me, bellowing. I slammed on the brakes and careened across the road, my tires screaming on the blacktop. I hit the curb, mounted the sidewalk, and, as the rage inside me took hold, I released the brake and stood on the gas pedal.

There was a shattering explosion. I was thrown forward in my seat and smashed my chest and forehead against the wooden wheel. All around me there were showers of jagged, sparkling, spinning shards of glass, shattering and bouncing off the hood. They were like the shafts of pain stabbing through my head and my chest. But somehow it all seemed to be happening to somebody else, somewhere else.

I shoved open the door and climbed out. There was an alarm bell jangling, lonely and ineffectual in the night. The Jag was half inside the bar. All around the hood was the shattered debris of glass, broken tables and chairs. I looked back down Zerega. I was six or seven hundred yards from the crime scene. And there was a bend in the road at the intersection with Randall. They would not have seen or heard anything.

The bar was still and silent after the explosion of glass. It was a one-story building that sprawled back and to the right from the bar. There would be an office. There would be a kitchen. There might be living accommodation. I pulled the Smith & Wesson from under my arm, cocked the hammer, and moved across the floor to the bar. There was a door behind it. I remembered Teddy had come out through there the afternoon we had come to talk to him. I lifted the flap, moved behind the bar, and stepped up to it. It was locked.

I selected the screwdriver from my Swiss Army knife, rammed it in the lock, and turned. By the dim light that filtered in through the plate glass windows, I saw a short passage. At the end of the passage I could make out a single door. There was no handle and no lock, but there was a spring-loaded arm at the top. My gut told me this was the kitchen. I inched forward and pulled the door open, holding it with my foot. Nothing happened. I crouched down and peered in. It was dark but for the odd reflection of cold blue light off steel pots and pans. I listened for movement or breathing. There was nothing.

I stood and flipped on the light. The kitchen was empty, but across the other side there was another door. In my mind's eye I could see the layout of the building. I was at the right-hand extreme of the one-story section of the block. After this, it was two stories, and I was pretty sure that when I opened the door I would be in a stairwell. A stairwell is a death trap. But on the other side of that death trap was Dehan. There was no doubt in my mind about that.

I opened the door and peered in. The light was on. It was a narrow, straight flight of stairs. On the right it was wall all the way up. On the left it opened out into what seemed to be a room or a large landing. I flattened myself against the wall with my .45 held at arm's length in both hands, aimed at the landing, and started moving up slowly, one step at a time. The steps were wood and made enough noise to start a zombie revolution, but I was committed and there was no going back. I kept climbing. My whole body was rigid, expecting to get shot at any moment. I realized I wasn't breathing. I exhaled and took another step.

It wasn't a landing. It was a room. It was stark and cold, with sparse, old furniture that exemplified the worst of the '80s. There was a single, large window on the right. The drapes were open and the glass was black. Beneath the window there was a TV. It was off, angled across the room to a couple of couches set at right angles to each other around a nasty pine coffee table with a glass top. Teddy was sitting on the couch facing me. He was frozen, staring wide-eyed. I aimed the gun at his head and moved up the rest of the stairs. He watched me without speaking.

A passage ran down to my left, opposite the TV. In the passage, there were two doors. The one at the far end I guessed was the bathroom; the one halfway down would be the bedroom. I looked back at Teddy. He looked terrified.

"Where is she?"

He didn't answer. His breathing became heavier and he swallowed.

"Where is she, Teddy?"

When he spoke his voice was a rasp. "Who?"

I stepped closer to him, stared hard into his eyes, studied the texture of his skin, noted the rise and fall of his chest. "You need to understand something, Teddy. Detective Dehan is not just my partner. She's the woman I love. I will do whatever I have to do to save her life. If I lose my job, go to jail for the rest of my life, that is fine by me. Where is she?"

He shook his head. "I don't know what you're talking about. What was that noise downstairs? It sounded like a bomb . . ."

I jerked my gun at him. "Stand up."

He got to his feet with his hands held at shoulder height. I waved him toward the passage. "The bedroom."

"What are you going to do?"

"I am going to blow your head off and ransack this building if you don't do what I say, Teddy. I have probably already lost my job. Don't push me any further!"

"Okay, okay . . . Stay calm. This is all a misunderstanding. I will cooperate."

He inched around the coffee table and moved toward the bedroom. I stayed close. He stopped in front of the door. "I'm going to open it, okay?"

"Do it."

He turned the handle and eased it open, then reached in and flipped on the light. "Shall I go in?" He raised his hands again.

"Go in."

He went in a few steps and I followed. It was as sparse and cold as the living room. The bed was made. There was no room under it for anything. There was a small wardrobe. I said, "Open it," but I knew she wasn't in there. He opened it and there were just a few shirts, pants, and jackets.

I could feel my heart pounding, close to panic. My belly was burning. I fought to keep control, to try and understand. "The bathroom."

He nodded, hurried to the bathroom door, and pushed it open. There was an airing cupboard, which he opened without being told. It was empty, as was the half-size bath. I growled at him, "Where is she, Teddy?"

"I swear to God I don't know what you're talking about, Detective!"

I felt a chill creep over my skin. I was terrified at what I was about to do. My voice wasn't my own. It was cold and quiet. "I am going to count to three. Then I start shooting. Where is she?"

His eyes were wide. I saw his pupils contract, and now his skin went pale and pasty. "There is nowhere else in the house! What else can I show you? She isn't here!"

"One . . ."

His voice began to rise. "What can I do? Tell me! For God's sake! I haven't got her! You can see . . ."

"Two . . ."

"*She isn't here! For Christ's sake! How can I convince you . . . ?*"

"Three."

I leveled the gun at his head. He screamed, "*Wait! The cellar!*"

I paused.

"Where we keep the beer barrels. If I show you, and she's not there, will you believe me? I don't know what else I can do. You've made a mistake."

"Shut up. Show me the cellar."

He moved past me to the stairs and I followed him down. We went through the kitchen and out to the darkness of the bar. The streetlamps gleamed eerily off the shattered glass and the Jag sitting there, with its dark windows and the door hanging open. He stared at the scene of wreckage and chaos with his mouth open. "Sweet Jesus," he said. "You're insane."

I snarled, "You'd better believe it. The cellar."

He stared at me, swallowed, and moved to a door that stood beside the bathrooms and was marked *Private*. In the distance I could hear sirens. He fumbled in his trouser pocket and pulled out a bunch of keys. I watched his hands as he slipped one of the keys in the lock and opened the door. It gave onto a small, narrow landing. He hit the switch and the light revealed a short flight of wooden steps that led down to a concrete floor. There I could just make out a stack of steel barrels.

"Go down."

He nodded and climbed down the stairs. At the bottom he backed up a little and watched me follow. I stood for a moment, looking around. There were stacks of crates: soft drinks, bottled beer, water. There were stacks of twelve-packs of cans, cartons of wine, and against the far wall a wooden wine rack stacked with dusty bottles.

I watched him a moment. He swallowed three times in rapid succession. He looked like he might start crying. I gave something that might have been a rueful smile. He shook his head and spread his hands. "You can see she's not here. Honest to God, Detective. I have no idea where she is."

I nodded. After a moment I said, "Teddy's Late-Night Bar."

He blinked.

"Your Australian barman was worried that we were after your license, because you stay open after you're supposed to close most nights."

He went very still. "We close the door. Just a few regulars shooting the breeze."

I took a couple of steps into the room, staring around me. "Tonight you closed early. By eleven thirty, when I arrived to see Wayne, you were shut. What made you close early, Teddy?"

He didn't answer for a moment. Then he said, "They're not worth it, Detective. Even the sweet ones are just whores."

My head exploded. The pain was shattering. Then a concrete wall hit me in the face and I knew I had fallen to the floor. A voice in my head told me not to let go of my gun, but a crushing pain in my hand made me cry out and I felt him levering the pistol from my fingers.

"Get up."

I looked up at him.

He was expressionless. There was no anger and no fear. He said again, "Get up."

I got to my knees. My hand was throbbing. The room swayed and rocked and I thought for a moment I might vomit. I steadied myself on a crate of beer.

He said, "That'll do fine."

I pushed myself to my feet. "If I'm going to die," I said, "I won't do it on my knees."

He snorted. It might have been a laugh.

I said, "Is Dehan alive? Have you killed her?"

He nodded. "Yes, but don't worry. You'll be joining her soon. I've never killed a man before. It'll be a new experience. A cop too. Two cops in one night. That's something."

I felt empty. It was as though the floor fell away from under my feet. We don't realize it, but we all live with pictures of our past and our future crowding our minds. The moments, hours, days, and even years that have passed and are to come are permanent occupants of our minds. They give our lives coherence and meaning. In that one, brief instant, all of my future moments disintegrated. My future, my life, lost its meaning. All I could do was stare at him and try to make sense of what he had said. It had been a throwaway comment, but with it, with that casual ease, he had thrown away Dehan's life, and mine with it.

Dehan was dead.

NINETEEN

He pointed at the wine rack. "It's not as sophisticated as it looks." He gave an almost apologetic laugh. "All I did was take the door off the annex and put some casters on the wine rack. Give it a push."

I frowned at him. "Is she in there?"

He nodded and grinned. "Wayne likes his spot by the river. I prefer it here. It's . . ." He shrugged. "I don't know, more cozy. Push."

It was unreal. I felt that reality was slipping away from me. I shook my head. "Am I going to see her . . . ?"

He raised his eyebrows high on his forehead and smiled. "Yeah! Go on. Push."

It was too much for my brain to grasp. She was just a few feet away from me, on the other side of the wine rack. Every instinct in my body told me to go to her. But I had seen many times what strangulation does to somebody, and to see Dehan like that was unimaginable. All I had was the past: her looking at me from behind her shades, tying up her hair behind her head, raising her sunglasses to squint at me with that beautiful trace of a smile. I needed to preserve those memories, but I also needed to be close to her, however she looked now.

I moved to the wine rack and pushed. It rolled easily to the side, revealing a gaping door with an old, peeling frame. There was a soiled mattress on the floor, a short coil of green nylon cord, a chair. Dehan was not there.

I felt a hard shove in my back and I staggered forward. I turned, knowing what was coming next: the crack of the Smith & Wesson, the crushing impact of the hot slug on my chest, the burning, searing pain. I had felt it before, but this time it would be terminal.

There was a scream. It filled the small room. It was like a banshee exploding from the gates of hell. I saw the muzzle of the pistol pointing at me. I saw it spit fire and kick. At the same time I saw Dehan, tall, lanky, and wild, leaping at Teddy through the doorway, gripping the barrel of the automatic with her left hand and pummeling his belly with her right fist.

Next thing, she had levered the weapon from his fingers and smashed her right foot into his gut. He staggered back and crashed into a stack of red Coke crates, spilling them and shattering them in a spreading pool of foaming black liquid.

I said, "Dehan . . ." but my throat was too tight to let the word out.

She threw the gun on the floor. It fired, and I stared at it for what seemed like an hour but was less than a second as a plume of dust erupted in slow motion from the wall, where the slug had buried itself. I looked back at Dehan. She had her fists balled and was advancing on Teddy, who was crawling back-ward, trying to get to his feet. I saw blood trickling down his arm from where he had fallen on the shattered bottles. And, as he struggled away from her, I saw the jagged glass edge of a broken bottle neck.

I said, "Dehan, no, wait . . ."

But it was like a nightmare where you need to call out, but your throat is paralyzed. He scrambled to his feet and rushed her, swinging the cruel glass blade at her face. She weaved back and it missed her. Three jabs followed into his face, left, right, left, and she was roaring at him, "*Come on! You want to strangle me, you piece of shit? Come on! Do it!*"

He was bleeding from the nose and his eyes were wild. He stormed at her. I watched the blade miss her again by an inch as she delivered a right cross to his jaw. His leg wobbled and he staggered back three steps. She screamed at him again. "*Come on! What's wrong with you? You're the big man! You're the killer! You get off killing women! Come on! Kill me!*"

Upstairs I heard the wail of sirens, loud. They slowed, seemed to stab the air a couple of times. I snapped out of my trance. It had been just a couple of seconds. But it was a couple of seconds too long. I bent, picked up the pistol, and stepped out. I aimed the gun at Teddy and said, "Freeze. It's over. Put down the bottle."

Dehan glared at me. There was rage and resentment in her eyes. She wanted to take him. I ignored her and focused on Teddy. He was swaying and panting. He was still holding the broken bottle neck. I said, "Drop it, Teddy. Let it go. Lie facedown on the floor. It's over. Wayne is dead. We know everything."

He blinked. "Wayne?"

"He's on his way to the ME right now. They've seen my car. They're coming in. Put it down, Teddy."

He frowned. "*Wayne?*"

I coughed, gathered my voice, and shouted, "*Down here! In the cellar! Detectives Stone and Dehan!*"

Then I saw Teddy's face and I knew it was too late. It twisted into an ugly mask and he screamed. It was not a word. It was a primal, bestial, terrible noise and he rushed Dehan. I saw her eyes go wide and her mouth open. I fired at his head and watched the slug explode in red dust against the wall. By the time I'd pulled back the hammer again he was on her. The bottle plunging in, in a low thrust at her belly.

It was too fast to follow, too fast for thought. She had stepped to her left. The bottle had torn her blouse, but she was behind him now. His wrist was in her right hand, but her left arm was in a lock around his neck, and in an instant her right hand had released his wrist and was pressing the back of his head. She jerked and he went limp. She let go of him and he dropped to the floor in a strangely unnatural heap.

She stared at me. She said, automatically, "I did it without thinking. I had to stop him."

I nodded. "He had to be stopped."

I stepped over to her and put my arms around her, whispering over and over, to her and to myself, "*You're alive. Dear God, you're alive.*"

I felt her arms around my waist, squeezing tight, and she started to sob, warm, living tears into my shoulder. On the wooden stairs I heard the tramp of feet, and the inspector's voice shouting, "*John? Carmen? Are you there?*"

I ignored him. I just held her, and a moment later I heard his voice again, no longer shouting but gasping, "Dear God, what in the name of hell . . . ?"

I kept my eyes firmly closed and whispered again, "*Thank God you're alive . . .*"

EPILOGUE

THE INSPECTOR HAD HIS WINDOW OPEN. THE SKY WAS very fresh and blue, and the birds in the plane trees and the oaks on Story Avenue were getting a little overexcited. But it was okay. They were getting a kick out of being alive, and that was something I could relate to just then.

I wasn't sitting at the desk. Today I was an honored guest in his office, so I had one of his blue armchairs under the window, and a cool breeze was touching my face. Dehan had another armchair and the inspector was watching me from his big black leather seat, with a small frown of what I like to think was admiration.

"Well, John, I guess we all owe you an apology. You were right and we were all wrong. But, what I don't understand is . . . well . . ." He made an elaborate shrug, opened his eyes wide, and concluded, ". . . *anything!*"

Dehan smiled at me. "I have to say I'm pretty confused too. Who was doing the killing? Was it Jimmy, Wayne, or Teddy? Or all three?"

Before I could answer the inspector nodded and added, "And how did you *know*?"

I took a deep breath. "Well, the point is, as I kept telling

Dehan, most of the time I didn't know. I had the feeling right from the start that we were being maneuvered through a rat's maze toward a conclusion that Wayne wanted us to reach. And it seemed pretty obvious to me that, if that was the conclusion he wanted us to reach, it was the wrong conclusion. So, I *didn't* know, but everybody else thought they did know."

He made a face like a shrug and said, "There were things that troubled you from the start. Yet, Wayne seemed to answer those doubts..."

I nodded. "Wayne was smart. If he hadn't been so self-obsessed..."

The inspector glanced at a file on his desk. "His therapist at Rikers said he was a narcissistic sociopath."

"Yeah, that's no surprise. If he had directed his attention more to what he was doing and less to how he looked and sounded when he was doing it, he might actually have achieved something. He enjoyed the game of playing with the cops and feeling he was smarter than us.

"But he was sloppy and lazy. For a start, the place where he said he lay and watched the murder take place made no sense. There was a comfortable, grassy knoll where he could have lain and been invisible from the road. And if you come through that gate, as he said he did, the path takes you right to that spot. There was no reason for him to go and lie on those rocks and prickly bushes."

I paused, gathering my thoughts. "The fact that he then went to the trouble of explaining it, when it simply made no sense, told me he had gone away and thought it through and decided he *needed* to explain it to me. That meant one thing and one thing only, he was manipulating us. So I had to ask myself the question."

The inspector frowned and nodded. "Why would he want to manipulate us? I see."

I shook my head and saw Dehan smile. I said, "No, I try not to ask why, Inspector. Why is too open. I asked myself, what:

What would make him try to manipulate us? When you ask it like that, the answer leaps out at you."

Dehan raised a hand. "Hang on, Stone. Aren't we getting a bit too rarified here? He was simply covering the fact that he had been at the very spot where Angela died. He was covering the fact that he killed her."

"Sure, and that is true. But it leads you back to the very first question. What made him tell us he had information in the first place? If he'd just kept his mouth shut nobody would ever have suspected he was there at all. A couple of years and he would have been out and nobody the wiser. The question was, what would drive him to tell us he had information in the first place, connect himself with the murders, but make it seem he was a witness?"

She made a face and grunted. "Yeah, that was the circle I was trapped in."

"He needed us to know that he was there. He made that very clear from the start. And the fact that he lied about the place where he witnessed it from made it clear to me that he had actually been on the grassy knoll, either killing her himself, or watching it." I sighed. "Now, here is where it got a bit tricky. I began to feel there had to be more than one person involved. If he was just protecting himself, why draw attention to himself at all? He would only place himself at the scene if he was confident he could put somebody else in the frame."

I paused and looked at them. They were both looking a little lost, but nodding. I went on.

"He confirmed this when we took him to the river and he showed us where the purse was. That was important for a couple of reasons. First of all, he needed to get up close to find the spot. How could he possibly do that if he had witnessed the hiding of the purse from almost a hundred yards away at night? There was only one way he could have known so precisely where it was—and recognize the spot by a close inspection—if he had put it there himself." I paused and smiled. "To quote Sir Walter Scott, 'Oh, what a tangled web we weave, when first we practice to deceive!'

It's a web that tends to trap the deceiver sooner than the deceived. Because, when he realized that he had to explain this to me as well, he told me that it was he, and not Jimmy, who had hidden the purse. You remember he said he had done this to secure some kind of insurance."

Dehan was very quiet. The inspector said, "Yes, I remember, on your recording."

I gave a small laugh. "So how is it that his prints were not on Angela's purse but Jimmy's were?" They both frowned. I went on, "Okay, follow me here. Jimmy has handled the purse, at the bar or wherever. His prints are on it. He takes Angela to the river. He kills her. The patrol boat shows up. He runs. Wayne goes to the body, picks up the purse, leaving his own prints on it, and then what? He wipes them off? How does he do that without wiping Jimmy's prints off? So that means . . . ?" I looked at them both. "He used gloves. So, what? He went to the river to smoke a joint and look at the stars, chose the most uncomfortable, inconvenient spot he could find, and, in May, happened to take a pair of gloves along with him." I shook my head. "No, it's absurd, his prints should have been on the purse, and they weren't, which meant this was another part of the manipulation."

Dehan said, "I should have seen that."

I had no answer. I agreed with her. So I went on.

"And that led me to a disturbing conclusion. As I said before, if Wayne was willing to admit that he had been at the scene and hidden the purse, he had to have some kind of ace up his sleeve, somebody to put in the frame, to prove that *he* had not committed the murder.

"To begin with, the question, why would he implicate himself if he was guilty, would be enough. But by this stage, when he actually knew the location of her purse, he needed something more. He needed proof positive that somebody else—the person he was framing—had done it. There was only one way to do that." I glanced at Dehan. "You remember I told you I had a bad feeling something terrible was going to happen?"

She nodded. "Cherry Pie, Noelia Gomez."

"Her murder was intended to confirm his story, but it actually confirmed my theory. There was somebody else, an accomplice. The pressure to get the killer caught, to get Wayne's testimony, was such that you overlooked the obvious ways in which this was not the same MO. The key, central, defining characteristic of the previous murders was missing."

Dehan sighed. "He didn't dump her in the river. It crossed my mind several times, but everything else . . ."

I shook my head. "No. Not that. The point is that Angela, Rosario, and Sonia—and who knows how many more—were murdered *because* they were nice, demure, respectable, middle-class Catholic girls. He would never have preyed on prostitutes. And that meant that Noelia died simply to put Jimmy firmly in the frame. *That* is why she was not thrown into the river.

"The river had proved to be a very effective way of getting rid of forensic evidence. But now they wanted to preserve it. This body had to be found. So, instead of taking her the short two-hundred-yard walk across the playing fields to the river, where he could dump her in the water, he took her five hundred yards into the woods, where her body would be found in a very short time. Not only that, but he went to all the trouble of wearing gloves so as not to leave his fingerprints, yet kindly donated his semen so that we could get a DNA profile on him. That murder was totally out of character with Angela's killer. It was obviously a frame."

They both looked embarrassed. The inspector nodded. "The results came back. It was Jimmy's DNA. As you predicted."

I shrugged. "Jimmy Fillmore was a nice guy who was a little simple. Like Wayne and Teddy, he had a thing about Hispanic women. But unlike Wayne and Teddy, he didn't want to kill them, he just wanted to sleep with them. He didn't have much success, he was described more than once as the kind of guy you just didn't notice, so, often as not, he resorted to prostitutes. This was something that both Wayne and Teddy knew.

"So they paid Noelia, perhaps Zena—who knows?—to keep

the contents of the condom." I turned to Dehan. "You wondered why I asked where the semen was on Cherry's clothes. Her skirt was rumpled up under her ass. There was no way the semen could have got there unless it was placed. It was stupid to go to the trouble of not leaving prints, then leave his semen and not dump her in the river, as he had done with all his other victims."

The inspector sighed. "We should have seen it." He frowned. "But why Jimmy? Why pick on Jimmy Fillmore?"

"It was one of those unfortunate coincidences, a series of unfortunate events, if you like. Wayne came to New York from Arizona, maybe he was running, maybe he was drifting, maybe we'll never know. He said he didn't like New York, but something made him stay. That something was that he happened to meet a fellow traveler, Teddy, somebody who shared his own peculiar fantasies. Another thing we will probably never know is whether either of them had killed before, or whether it was their friendship that gave them the impetus to turn their fantasies into reality. But one of the things that struck me was that, when I asked Teddy if he knew Wayne, he said he had never met him. It stuck somewhere in the back of my mind. Yet Wayne talked about Teddy as though they were old friends." I sighed. "I was very slow to see that, even though it was staring me in the face.

"Trouble was, by then it had become urgent for me to find Jimmy, because I was aware that if Wayne and his invisible accomplice had set Jimmy up for the frame, obviously, they would have to kill him before we got to him."

Dehan raised both hands. "Slow down. You still haven't explained, why Jimmy in the first place?"

"Yeah . . ." I sighed again. It had been a couple of days, but my bruises still ached and I still had a throb in my head. "Jimmy was a surprisingly complex character, and he was invaluable to Wayne and Teddy. To most people he was the classic Mr. Cellophane: Mr. Invisible. That was how Pam described him, and how Teddy described him. But when you did stop to look at him, he was good-looking: he had those big brown eyes that so many women find attractive, and—and this was crucial—he was sincere and vulnerable. He was a fantasist, a dreamer, but he had no malice in him. He was one of life's natural victims. And *that* was very appealing to one particular type of young woman.

"We'll never know exactly how it went down. But at some point Teddy or Wayne, or both of them, realized that Jimmy was a magnet for those very girls that they were attracted to—that they fantasized about killing. Girls who would disdain Wayne's brutishness and Teddy's middle-aged, uncle-ish looks would find Jimmy adorable. They would want to mother him. So they began to encourage it. Those were the photographs we saw. Friendly, fun evenings at the local family bar.

"And Wayne fancied himself as a bit of a natural psychologist. Maybe he did have a low, cunning grasp of people's most basic motivations. So my guess is he began to encourage Jimmy's fantasies and even feed them. And Jimmy began to pass these on to the girls. Remember, these girls came from sheltered backgrounds and were very naïve. If Jimmy told them his dad was a TV producer making him work his way through college, and Teddy and Wayne backed him up and vouched for him, they might well believe him. It wouldn't be hard then to lure them into a trap." I shook my head. "Where they would never follow Wayne or Teddy—to an apartment, to some rendezvous—they might follow Jimmy, in all his simple innocence, without question. He was quite simply a perfect bait for the kind of girls that Wayne and Teddy liked to prey on."

Dehan nodded. "You kept asking me if Wayne was attractive. I kept on saying, to some women he would be, but not to the Angelas and Rosarios of this world. Jimmy was cute, he lacked something, but like you say, to a nice, maternal family girl, he could be attractive."

"Four things clinched it for me at Jimmy's apartment: the fact that Jimmy shot himself with his left hand, which was simply impossible; the fact that none of the trophies in the box related to Rosario or Sonia; the two glasses . . ."

The inspector cut in: "They had, as you suspected, Wayne's prints on them." He frowned. "And Frank said to tell you there was rum in his belly."

I nodded. "And the lipstick."

Dehan narrowed her eyes. "You keep talking about lipstick. What is it with the lipstick?"

I smiled. "One of them, Wayne or Teddy"—I shrugged—"perhaps both, was fixated with kissing and lipstick. We will eventually find the true trophies, and they will be the lipsticks. Maybe then we'll get a real idea of how many girls they killed between them. All the girls had extensive bruising on their lips. Even Noelia, who was not the perfect profile for them, had her lipstick badly smeared and her lips bruised. Wayne's description of Jimmy killing Angela focused almost obsessively on the kissing. And the one thing that was missing from Angela's purse and from Noelia's purse was the lipstick. They were two wicked, cruel men who hungered for a maternal woman's kiss. We can only guess at what drove them to that depravity. Betrayal?" I shrugged again. "Teddy's last words to me before he cracked me over the head, 'They are not worth it. Even the sweet ones are whores.'" I shrugged. "I guess once they yielded to Jimmy's advances, that branded them as whores in Wayne and Teddy's minds, and that sentenced them to death."

Dehan said, "If he had just sat out his sentence . . ."

I smiled. "But he was vain. That was one of the things that I began to realize early on. We kept asking, if he was the killer, why would he draw attention to himself? Well, the answer is simple. He was a narcissist. He wanted his deal to get out of prison, sure, but he also wanted to rub it in our faces that he was killing girls and getting away with it."

The inspector nodded for a long moment, big, slow nods. "A master class in detection, Stone. Very impressive. Well, I said it before and things went a bit pear-shaped. But I certainly think you have earned a good few days' rest."

I nodded. "I think we are going to need it, sir."

THAT EVENING we sat in Zack's Bar & Grille in Stonington, sipping dry martinis and waiting for our fresh seafood starter, feeling bruised, ragged, but healing and happy. Dehan had been watching me for a while. With that smile she gets when she thinks she knows what I'm thinking.

"So," she said. "You didn't drive me all the way out here just to eat seafood. What's the surprise?"

I raised an eyebrow and smiled back. "I thought tomorrow we could cross over to Fishers Island and spend a couple of days doing absolutely nothing."

"Uh-huh . . ." She bobbed the olive in her martini a couple of times. "That's nice. But that's not it either."

I gave my head a little shake. "You're right." I hesitated. "This may come as a bit of a surprise, Dehan, but I'm actually not a big risk-taker. I'm pretty cautious. I take things very much one step at a time."

She was frowning hard. "That doesn't come as a surprise at all, Stone. I've known that for a long time. Where is this going?"

I heaved a big sigh and took a sip of martini, wishing I'd ordered a whiskey. "I would never do anything, Dehan, to jeopardize our . . ." I spread my hands. "Our whateveritis."

"Our whateveritis?"

"Yeah."

"Calling it that is a pretty big risk, Stone."

"I know. And I don't want to call it that anymore."

Her frown deepened. "What are you saying?"

I looked down at the tabletop, then looked into her eyes. "I almost told you once before, outside Teddy's." I gave my head a small shake. "I can't do this anymore, Dehan. You are young, beautiful, *modern*. I am an old dinosaur. When Teddy told me he had killed you, it almost killed me. It's too much. I need to end this . . . *whateveritis*."

"*End* it?"

"Yeah. I want to call it something else. I want to call *you* something else. I don't want either of us to die without my having called you my wife. I think that is what I most want in the world. Carmen, will you please marry me?"

I watched the tears spring into her eyes. She frowned, then gave a small laugh. "You son of a bitch," she said. "Of course I will!"

Don't miss MURDER MOST SCOTTISH. The riveting sequel in the Dead Cold Mystery series.

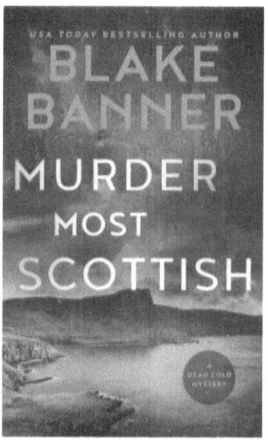

Scan the QR code below to purchase MURDER MOST SCOTTISH.

Or go to: righthouse.com/murder-most-scottish

NOTE: flip to the very end to read an exclusive sneak peak...

DON'T MISS ANYTHING!

If you want to stay up to date on all new releases in this series, with this author, or with any of our new deals, you can do so by joining our newsletters below.

In addition, you will immediately gain access to our entire *Right House VIP Library,* which includes many riveting Mystery and Thriller novels for your enjoyment!

righthouse.com/email

(Easy to unsubscribe. No spam. Ever.)

ALSO BY BLAKE BANNER

Up to date books can be found at:
www.righthouse.com/blake-banner

ROGUE THRILLERS
Gates of Hell (Book 1)
Hell's Fury (Book 2)

ALEX MASON THRILLERS
Odin (Book 1)
Ice Cold Spy (Book 2)
Mason's Law (Book 3)
Assets and Liabilities (Book 4)
Russian Roulette (Book 5)
Executive Order (Book 6)
Dead Man Talking (Book 7)
All The King's Men (Book 8)
Flashpoint (Book 9)
Brotherhood of the Goat (Book 10)
Dead Hot (Book 11)
Blood on Megiddo (Book 12)
Son of Hell (Book 13)

HARRY BAUER THRILLER SERIES
Dead of Night (Book 1)
Dying Breath (Book 2)
The Einstaat Brief (Book 3)
Quantum Kill (Book 4)
Immortal Hate (Book 5)
The Silent Blade (Book 6)
LA: Wild Justice (Book 7)

Breath of Hell (Book 8)
Invisible Evil (Book 9)
The Shadow of Ukupacha (Book 10)
Sweet Razor Cut (Book 11)
Blood of the Innocent (Book 12)
Blood on Balthazar (Book 13)
Simple Kill (Book 14)
Riding The Devil (Book 15)
The Unavenged (Book 16)
The Devil's Vengeance (Book 17)
Bloody Retribution (Book 18)
Rogue Kill (Book 19)
Blood for Blood (Book 20)

DEAD COLD MYSTERY SERIES
An Ace and a Pair (Book 1)
Two Bare Arms (Book 2)
Garden of the Damned (Book 3)
Let Us Prey (Book 4)
The Sins of the Father (Book 5)
Strange and Sinister Path (Book 6)
The Heart to Kill (Book 7)
Unnatural Murder (Book 8)
Fire from Heaven (Book 9)
To Kill Upon A Kiss (Book 10)
Murder Most Scottish (Book 11)
The Butcher of Whitechapel (Book 12)
Little Dead Riding Hood (Book 13)
Trick or Treat (Book 14)
Blood Into Wine (Book 15)
Jack In The Box (Book 16)
The Fall Moon (Book 17)
Blood In Babylon (Book 18)
Death In Dexter (Book 19)
Mustang Sally (Book 20)

A Christmas Killing (Book 21)
Mommy's Little Killer (Book 22)
Bleed Out (Book 23)
Dead and Buried (Book 24)
In Hot Blood (Book 25)
Fallen Angels (Book 26)
Knife Edge (Book 27)
Along Came A Spider (Book 28)
Cold Blood (Book 29)
Curtain Call (Book 30)

THE OMEGA SERIES
Dawn of the Hunter (Book 1)
Double Edged Blade (Book 2)
The Storm (Book 3)
The Hand of War (Book 4)
A Harvest of Blood (Book 5)
To Rule in Hell (Book 6)
Kill: One (Book 7)
Powder Burn (Book 8)
Kill: Two (Book 9)
Unleashed (Book 10)
The Omicron Kill (Book 11)
9mm Justice (Book 12)
Kill: Four (Book 13)
Death In Freedom (Book 14)
Endgame (Book 15)

ABOUT US

Right House is an independent publisher created by authors for readers. We specialize in Action, Thriller, Mystery, and Crime novels.

If you enjoyed this novel, then there is a good chance you will like what else we have to offer! Please stay up to date by using any of the links below.

Join our mailing lists to stay up to date -->
righthouse.com/email
Visit our website --> righthouse.com
Contact us --> contact@righthouse.com

 facebook.com/righthousebooks
 x.com/righthousebooks
 instagram.com/righthousebooks

EXCLUSIVE SNEAK PEAK OF...

MURDER MOST SCOTTISH

CHAPTER 1

WE'D TOUCHED DOWN IN EDINBURGH AT 7:10 A.M. local time, collected a large, characterless vehicle from the car hire centre, and, resisting the temptation to explore Edinburgh, we took the M90, crossed the Firth of Forth over the spectacular Forth Road Bridge as the sun climbed over the North Sea, and headed north, toward the wild and remote north coast of Scotland, in the Scottish Highlands.

I drove first, and Dehan sat back and watched the strange, conflicted landscape that was at once gray, drab, and postindustrial, and wild and green and timelessly Celtic. Pretty soon we were outside town and driving through picture-book rolling fields and hedgerows under very blue skies with lazy, whipped cream clouds.

Dehan was staring this way and that with slightly narrowed eyes, her aviators perched on top of her head. She said, suddenly, "Somebody shrunk New England."

I smiled. "Your first glimpse of the world outside the USA, Dehan."

She frowned at me. "You know, if you keep calling me by my surname, you'll have to call me Stone. We'll have to call *each other* Stone. That could become confusing."

I was quiet for a bit, smiling to myself. "I won't deny," I said, "that I get a foolish kick out of calling you Mrs. Stone."

She raised an eyebrow and smiled too.

I continued, "I know people don't get it, but I figure that's their problem, not mine. Either way, and even if it seems contradictory, you will always be Dehan." I shrugged. "That's just who you are to me."

"It is contradictory, but that's cool. How long is this drive?"

"Six or seven hours, through some of the most remote, beautiful landscapes this side of the Atlantic. That gets us to John o'Groats . . ."

"John o'Groats. That is some name."

"The most northerly part of Great Britain. Midsummer they get only a couple of hours of darkness at night. From there we drive west for four miles to the ferry at Gills, and from there . . ."

"The ferry to the island of Gordon's Swona, another eight miles by sea. And from there, another mile by road to the castle. So total . . . ?"

"Maybe nine hours. We should arrive at teatime."

"Teatime?"

I grinned. "It's a great institution: tuna and cucumber sandwiches cut into bite-size triangles, biscuits, rich fruitcake . . ."

"And tea."

"And tea. It tastes different when they make it here."

She was quiet for a moment, watching me. "You ever going to tell me what your connection is with this place?"

"Yup."

She waited, watching me. Finally she said, "Stone . . . ?"

"While we're here, I promise." Before she could answer, I changed the subject. "But you know what? I never heard of Castle Gordon. How did you find it?"

She shrugged and spread her hands. "I'm a detective. I detect. It's what I do."

"What did you google?"

"Whiskey, remote, castle."

"So naturally you wound up with a list of remote Scottish castles converted to hotels."

"This one was the remotest of the lot. It's only been a hotel for the last couple of years, though the Gordon family bought it back in 1980."

I glanced at her, curious. "Bought it back?"

She shifted in her seat, with her back half against the door. "Yeah, it was bought by an American with Scottish roots. His family were from the area and his ancestors owned, and then lost, the castle. His family made a lot of money during the Civil War and the drive west, and he made even more during the sixties and seventies, then moved here in the early eighties and bought the castle, which he claimed had belonged to his great-great-whatevers. The place is now run by his grandson, Charles Gordon Jr."

I was quiet for a bit, enjoying the landscape and the fresh summer breeze gently battering me through the window. After a moment I said, half to myself, "Great-great-whatevers. I remember a restaurant in Colorado that specialized in those. They called them Colorado oysters."

"Funny guy. So how long were you here, Stone? And where and when?"

"I was in London, for eighteen months, about fifteen years ago. It was supposed to be six months as part of an exchange program between the NYPD and Scotland Yard. I was in my early thirties. They kept telling me to go back to New York, and I kept finding ways to extend my stay for another six months."

"Huh." She was pensive for a moment, suspecting she already knew the answer to the question she hadn't asked yet. "What made you want to stay?"

I shrugged. "I was enjoying myself. I made some good friends. . ."

She interrupted, "And you were in love."

I nodded. "Yeah, I was in love. But that was fifteen years ago."

"What happened?"

I made a face that told her to stop asking questions and said,

"What happened? Fifteen years went by, I met a nosy, wiseass cop with a bad attitude and married her. That's what happened."

She looked away. "Fine, don't tell me."

"I'll tell you." I shrugged again. "There's not a lot to tell. There's no great secret, Dehan. I just don't want to talk about it on the first day of our honeymoon."

"I get it."

We drove on for another three or four hours, had lunch in a country pub, and finally reached Gills, at the northernmost part of Scotland, at three o'clock that afternoon. Gills turned out to be not so much a town as a loose collection of houses gathered around an intersection. There was no post office, town hall, or local store or pub that I could see. So we wound down a narrow road between rugged, green hills toward a gunmetal-gray sea, highlighted with liquid silver, that stretched out cold and deadly toward the Arctic.

We stopped on a concrete quay outside a quaint cottage with chimneys at either end that claimed to be the Ferry Terminal and climbed out to stand gazing at the misty horizon. I pointed out to sea, where large clouds were building in the far north. "Only four hundred miles, Dehan, and you're in Iceland."

She gave a small, involuntary shudder. "That's like from New York to Cleveland." She glanced up at me. "Isn't Iceland in the Arctic Circle?"

"Just outside, but you get the midnight sun there in June, and twenty-four hours of darkness in December. Here, in this part of Scotland, it gets dark about midnight, and starts getting light at about two thirty."

"I guess we went north, huh, Stone?"

I smiled. "We've still a way to go."

We crossed the bare concrete and pushed through the door into the ferry terminal. There was a man in a heavy white sweater behind a melamine counter. He looked like he'd once tried to shave but busted the razor and gave up on a hopeless task. There was the blackened, withered remains of a roll-up hanging from the corner of his mouth. He watched us come in with expression-less, pale eyes and waited for us to talk.

I essayed a smile against my better judgment and said, "We'd like to cross to Gordon's Swona . . ."

He interrupted me and said something that sounded like, "Tharteh eet poonds fer th'car, suxteen fer the missus an' suxteen fer yersen."

I narrowed my eyes, pretty sure I'd understood, nodded, and said, "That's fine."

He rang it up on his register, with small flakes of ash falling from his dead cigarette. Then he looked at me slow and steady and there was evil humor in his eyes. "Suventeh poonds."

I glanced at the register to make sure I'd understood and handed over two fifties. He took his time getting my change and handing it back. Then he leered. "Uz et the Gordon Castle yir aweetah?"

I nodded. "Yes."

"Yir ferry'll moor within the hoor, gang t'thend of yon peer an'll nay be long."

I nodded again. "Thanks."

As I turned and opened the door, he added, "Ut was plowe-trery thus mornin' and a haar in from th'east thus afternoon. Tull be mochie afore the gloaming, fer-sure, an' nay doot there'll be a fair gailleann by t'morrah."

Dehan blinked furiously at him. I nodded one last time, thanked him, and returned to the car.

"What was that, Stone? Was that English?"

"With a liberal dose of Scots Gaelic. I think he said there'd be a storm tomorrow."

"You understood him?"

I didn't answer; instead I fired up the car. Fortunately the signs were in plain English and I drove to the loading point where I figured the ferry would dock, then stopped and thought for a moment.

I turned to her. "Tull be mochie afore the gloaming. It will be muggy before dusk. An' nay doot there'll be a fair gailleann by t'morrah. And no doubt there will be a fair gale, or storm, by tomorrow. Weather here is pretty unpredictable."

She stared at me for a long moment without expression. Then she said with a hint of disapproval, "You're a remarkable man, Stone."

The sea was flat and almost milky in consistency. The crossing took an hour and was unremarkable, except that the views from the deck, of the Isle of Stroma to the west and Orkney to the north, were extraordinary. There was a desolation about the beauty of the place that was not quite like anywhere else. At one point Dehan shook her head, squinting into the sea breeze, fingering her long hair from her face. "I never imagined England like this . . ."

I laughed. "Don't let them hear you say that. This is not England. Scotland is a country in its own right. In some ways it is closer to Scandinavia than it is to England."

She frowned and shook her head. "It's so . . . *remote!*"

"Yup. And you have brought us to the most remote part, of the remote part."

She took hold of my arm and squeezed it. "Good. No inspector, no Mo, no distractions, no cold cases for two long, wonderful weeks."

We stood like that for a while, enjoying the strange, peaceful desolation. It had turned warm and close, and Dehan ran her fingers over her brow. Then she gave a small laugh. "He was right!"

I smiled at her. "Hm?"

"The guy at the terminal. He said it would turn muggy in the afternoon . . ."

I did a fair imitation of his brogue. "Tull be mochie afore the gloaming, an' nay doot there'll be a fair gailleann by t'morrah."

She looked up into my face. "So we'll have a storm tomorrow? That means breakfast in bed and hot toddies in front of the fire."

"I'm not complaining. Bring it on."

We sighted Gordon's Swona twenty minutes later. It was a wedge-shaped island that rose dramatically out of the sea mist. The narrow end consisted of high cliffs and a relatively flat table-land towering some hundred and fifty or two hundred feet above the waves, and then sloping gently for about a mile and a half, or a little more, toward broad, rolling grasslands and white, sandy beaches. On the tableland, at the top of the cliffs, a spectacular castle stood silhouetted in the coppery afternoon light.

As we stood staring, the note of the engines changed and we began to slow, churning the water and nosing toward the beach where we could now see a small port with a long pier that had been built out of wood and concrete. Eventually, after some careful maneuvering, we eased to a halt, the apron ramp was dropped with a huge, metallic clang that threatened to take off the end of the dock, and, amid a lot of shifting, drifting, and grinding, we rolled out of the cargo hold and onto the concrete pier.

And then we stood by the car and watched as the ramp was raised, clattering and clanking, to its closed position. The ferry reversed away from the dock, turned, lumbering, and slowly took off north, toward the distant shadow of Orkney on the horizon.

Behind us, in the south, the mainland was no longer visible, but before us the road wound through gentle hills of green pasture, meadow flowers, and heather, where sheep and goats ruminated and watched us with saurian eyes, to a broad forest, perhaps a mile away, that climbed the slopes for perhaps another half mile toward the hazy silhouette of the castle on the hill. All around us, the air was rich with the smells of aromatic grasses and herbs—maybe lavender, rosemary, and thyme. It seemed very still. The only sounds were the lapping of the small waves on the shore and the lazy buzz of bees among the grass and flowers.

Ahead, about halfway up the slope, half a mile from the castle, we could just make out a small village among the woods by the road. It seemed to consist mainly of stone cottages and tall chimney stacks poking up among the trees.

I glanced at my watch. It was six o'clock, and though the light was definitely coppery and there was a feel of evening to the sultry air, the sun was still a good four hours or more from setting.

I smiled at Dehan. "Let's go."

It was a fifteen-minute drive, because though the speed limit on the island was 25 MPH, the road wended and wove in big loops, and in many parts it was rough and pitted. When we passed through the village, we saw that it consisted of a village green, a handful of houses, a two-story post office, and a picturesque pub called the Gordon Arms; and a moment later we were in the woods again, winding our way up the steep hill through tall pine trees that cast an eerie green light, until at last we broke out of the forest and onto the broad, flat, grassy tableland. There the road went straight, and ahead of us, tall and ancient, stood the castle, brooding, lowering over the dark expanse of the North Atlantic toward the Arctic Circle and the heavy, dark clouds that were gathering there.

As we drew closer, we could see that Castle Gordon was encircled by an ancient stone wall, perhaps eight feet high. But in many places that wall had crumbled over time, and where it had collapsed, leaving great gaps in the masonry, it had been replaced with hedges and trees, giving the vague impression that Nature was slowly winning in a war of attrition against Man.

The road entered the grounds of the castle through a large iron gate that stood open, and from the gate onward the road became the driveway. On either side of that drive there were well-tended lawns and formal gardens, and to the left there was a large topiary maze.

A butler in traditional dress and a page were waiting for us at the foot of the stone steps that led up to the main door. When we pulled up, the butler opened the door for Dehan and welcomed us to Gordon's Swona while the page took my keys to open the trunk, unload our luggage, and park the car. While he did that, I stood back and had a good look at the building. You could have described it as a horrific mixture of styles thrown together with a total disregard for esthetics or proportion, a monstrous affront to architecture and a grotesque stone pile. You could very well have described it like that, if you'd had no soul.

On the right-hand side, at the front, there was a massive, square, four-story solid stone tower with castellations at the top and narrow, gabled windows on the second, third, and fourth floors. On the ground floor, a leaded bay window overlooked yellow and red rosebushes, while dense ivy swarmed up the wall as far as the second floor.

The central body of the building was granite, with a gabled portico supported on ancient stone pillars, and a gabled slate roof with tall chimney pots. To my uneducated eye, it looked as though the tower was Victorian mock Elizabethan, where the main body was maybe two hundred years older, maybe seventeenth century. On the far left there was another wing in paler stone, running at right angles to the house. It was only three stories high, with small, narrow windows and battlements up top. That, I guessed, was what was left of the original castle. The overall effect was that of a messy jumble of rocks and styles, but somehow it came together and became a beautiful, ancient work of art.

"You coming?"

Dehan was standing on the granite steps smiling at me. The butler was at the door, holding it open, as though there was nothing else in the world he needed to be doing right then. The sun was bright, and the scent of the roses was strong on the air. For a moment it was a perfect, timeless scene. I smiled, said, "I'm coming," and stepped toward her, and as we climbed the steps together, a cloud moved across the sun, casting a deep shadow over the castle, and a clammy, muggy breeze touched my skin.

We stepped through the door, and the butler said, "Welcome to Castle Gordon."

CHAPTER 2

We stepped into a vaulted, Gothic entrance hall. The floor was tiled in a black-and-white checkerboard pattern, and a magnificent stone staircase rose directly in front of us, and then split in two to ascend, right and left, to a galleried first-floor landing. Immediately on our right was a reception desk, and coming out from behind it as we entered was a man in his early thirties in chinos and a blazer, with blond hair swept back from a face that was intelligent, but too kind to be handsome.

He held out a large, soft hand and smiled as we approached. "Mr. and Mrs. Stone, I imagine. How splendid that you could join us. We have a full house this summer."

There was no trace of an accent, and I figured he had been educated at an English boarding school. We shook hands and he added, as though we had asked, "Charles Gordon. My father insists on calling me Junior, because he is also Charles. So we call him Senior. He's an American, you know. Now!" He gave each of us a broad grin and held out his arms like he was about to hug us. "I imagine you will want to freshen up after a long journey. Brown will show you to your room, and we'll be having cocktails in the drawing room . . ." He gestured across the hall to a set of walnut doors. "At seven. Then you'll be able to meet our other charming guests. We'll be going in to dine at about half seven or eight."

Dehan frowned. "Half seven?" Then she grinned. "What's that, three thirty?"

Charles laughed.

I said, "Seven thirty, smart-ass. Thank you, Charles, that sounds perfect. I've heard you have an exceptional range of whiskeys."

"Second to none, old chap, and I'll guide you through them with great pleasure. I've put you in the tower, in the honeymoon suite. I trust you'll find it comfortable."

The honeymoon suite was everything you'd expect from a Hollywood rendition of a Scottish castle. There was a gigantic mahogany four-poster bed with drapes, there were gabled, leaded windows overlooking the formal gardens, a stone fireplace big enough to house a small family, and vast, bare wooden rafters overhead. The walls were oak paneled, and on the bedside table there was a silver bucket filled with ice, holding a bottle of Bollinger and two Edinburgh crystal glasses.

Once Brown had put our cases on the bed and left, Dehan stood looking around with a big smile all over the right side of her face. "Oh man," she said. "Stone."

I took off my jacket and she crossed the room to poke her head into the bathroom. "There is a freestanding tub, with clawed feet and gold taps." She turned and winked at me. "Open the champagne, big guy, we're going to have a bath, Scottish castle style . . ."

———

AN HOUR LATER, we joined the other guests in the drawing room.

The Gordon Castle was a boutique hotel. There was no pool, no bar, and no dining room in the usual sense of the word. More than staying at a hotel, it was like staying with a rich friend at his country manor. Instead of several hundred anonymous guests milling around a vast building in Florida, here we had just a handful of fellow guests who had cocktails in the drawing room, and lunched and dined with the family in the ancestral dining room. It was different, and it had sounded like exactly what Dehan and I needed.

The drawing room was big. The floors were wood, strewn with what looked like genuine Persian rugs, and to the right of the door as you went in, there was a huge granite fireplace. Right now there were several large logs burning in it. An eclectic collection of sofas and armchairs, standard lamps, and occasional tables were scattered around the room in an apparently random fashion that somehow managed to be homely and comfortable. Against the far wall, an elaborate credenza held an extensive collection of bottles, hand-cut decanters, and glasses. To the left of it, French windows stood open onto a stone terrace with steps down onto the lawns and the gardens.

There were a number of people standing and sitting, and they all turned to watch us come in. For a moment they looked like a bizarre frozen tableau from an early play by Agatha Christie: Charles Gordon was standing by the drinks, dressed in a tuxedo, holding a cocktail shaker. On the crimson-and-gold sofa directly in front of the fire was a woman who was still attractive in her midfifties. She had short, black hair and wore a long evening dress of deep blue satin, with a string of pearls around her neck. She had very red lipstick and regarded Dehan with wary eyes.

In an aquamarine armchair with wooden legs, also beside the fire, was another woman, blond, perhaps in her early sixties. She wore a low-cut white satin dress with a gash up to her thigh, exposing a leg that looked thirty years younger than she did.

A third woman stood by the French windows, smoking. She was younger than the other two, perhaps thirty. Her dress was mauve, and the gash, up to her hip, exposed a leg you had to try hard not to look at. She had hair that was wild, curly, and red, tied back in a mauve satin bow. Her face should have been pretty, but a spray of freckles and mischievous blue eyes made it more captivating than that.

Besides Charles, there were two other men in the room. One was standing beside the redhead. He was tall and strongly built, wearing what looked like an off-the-peg Italian suit. He had black hair and sullen eyes, which he was using to undress Dehan. I figured he was in his thirties.

The other was standing by the fire. Like Charles, he was wearing an evening suit and a bow tie. He was probably in his late fifties and had that stiff, brisk air that the British military brass all seem to acquire by osmosis.

They all smiled with varying degrees of sincerity, and Charles said in a loud voice, "Ah! You're here! Well done! Now, what will you have? Major, care to make the introductions?"

Before the major could get started, Dehan said, "Any whiskey you recommend, straight up. Stone will have the same."

The blonde in the aquamarine chair, with the low-cut white dress, turned out to be our hostess, Charles Jr.'s mother, Pamela. She smiled at me without moving, raised an eyebrow, and sipped her drink, then said, "How do you do, John?"

I caught something in her voice which I filed away under irrelevant gossip that might later be useful, and asked her how *she* did. Then the major gestured toward the woman on the sofa in the blue dress.

"Lady Jane Butterworth, Detective John Stone and his wife, Detective Carmen Stone."

She ignored Dehan but leaned forward and offered me her hand to kiss. "I don't use my title, I'm a committed socialist, you know," she said breathlessly, then laughed. "I hope you won't arrest me! Call me Bee, may I call you Stone? Such a *strong* name."

I told her I wouldn't and she could, and the major led us on to the couple at the French windows. "Dr. and Sally Cameron, very old friends of the family! Ian has his surgery opposite the pub in the village. Very handy, eh, Ian? And Sally owns the grocery store and runs the post office. Everyone does a bit of everything on Gordon's Swona, hay?"

The major laughed and the doctor looked at him with distaste. Sally stepped forward and kissed Dehan on the cheek while I shook the doctor's hand. I had seen friendlier eyes on great white sharks. We all asked each other how we did, and then the major laughed like he was telling a hilarious story and said, "And I am Major Reggie Hook, old friend of Charlie's, been coming here for years, ay, Charles?"

"Indeed!" Charles approached with two glasses of whiskey and handed them to us. With an enthusiasm that had more to do with wishful thinking than truth, he added, "We are all old friends here. Aren't we, Mummy?" Whatever Mummy was going to answer, he didn't give her a chance. He plowed on, "I think you'll like this single malt. It's from the local distillery and a bit of a hidden treasure. We have superb water here."

The thing continued in that vein for the next half hour. At first I worried that it would get on Dehan's nerves. I knew well that her tolerance of BS and small talk was limited, at best, but when I glanced at her, talking to Charles, I saw her eyes were alive and she was smiling. I also noticed Ian Cameron watching her. I didn't blame him. She was in a very simple, but very expensive black dress with no sleeves or shoulders, and a silver chain around her neck with a single amethyst. It all served to highlight her own beauty. I smiled, partly because she was mine, and partly because that very beauty hid the kick-ass, Bronx-bred bad attitude that was never very far below the surface.

Pamela stood, gave me a thin smile, and joined Dehan and her son. She gave Dehan a frigid once-over and said, "What an exquisite dress, but darling, are you in mourning? Who died?"

Dehan raised an eyebrow at her and smiled. "My tolerance for bullshit. It died a long time ago, but I'm still in mourning."

Charles burst out laughing. Dehan caught my eye, winked, and grinned.

Then the door opened, and I noticed several things all at once.

Dr. Cameron stiffened and his hostile face became even more hostile. His wife, whose side he had not left since we'd entered the room, also stiffened, but the expression on her face was anticipation, not hostility. Everybody else in the room went silent and stared, except Dehan, who caught my eye again with an unspoken question.

The man who entered the room was aware of the effect he had, and of his own magnificence. He was over six foot, but if he'd been four foot two he would not have looked any smaller. He had a powerful chest, a powerful jaw, and a mane of silver hair swept back from a large forehead. His nose was aquiline and his pale blue eyes were cruel and ruthless. He was a man born to be king in a world that no longer needed kings.

Charles moved forward. "Ah, Father, there you are. May I present Detective Carmen Stone . . ."

Charles Gordon Sr. ignored his son and moved in on Dehan like a hungry wolf moving in on an injured baby gazelle. His voice was deep and resonant, with clear traces of his Boston roots. "Detective? I'll wager most of the men you hunt down surrender willingly."

I saw the doctor turn away. Dehan shook her head. "No, most of them need a couple of slaps and their hands cuffed."

He laughed. "You make it sound so appealing."

"Yeah? The reality is a little different, Mr. Gordon. This is my husband, Detective John Stone."

He gave me the kind of look that all the women in the room were giving Dehan. There was enough acid in there right then to clean a ton of copper. He raised an eyebrow.

"Another detective? We had better all behave, then, hadn't we? Though you are, of course, outside your jurisdiction."

I stepped up and put my hand on Dehan's elbow. "*And* on our honeymoon," I added. "Thank you, by the way, for the champagne. We enjoyed it."

"Don't thank me." He said it like he meant it. "Thank my

son. And speaking of useless incompetence, Charles, am I not entitled to a drink in my own house?"

He pushed past me toward his son, who was hurrying to the drinks tray, and Pamela, Lady Jane, and Sally Cameron all seemed to be sucked into his wake, like seagulls trailing after a Spanish galleon in full sail.

"What will you have, Father?"

"Let me see . . ." He didn't so much say it as boom it. "Let me see! Shall I have something different to *what I have every single night*? Good lord, boy! Can you take the initiative on *nothing*? Not even a simple task like getting your father a drink?"

"Vodka martini it is! What a character!"

There was some simpering and giggling and I stepped out the French windows onto the terrace. The sun was low on the horizon and the evening light was turning a grainy copper. The shadows of the trees stretched long across the lawns, and above, the blue was turning dark. There was a closeness to the air, and you could almost taste the static electricity in the humid air.

Dehan came out after me and rested her ass on the ancient stone balustrade. She gave a small laugh. "We just stepped through the looking glass, but instead of winding up with Alice in Wonderland, we wound up in an Agatha Christie novel."

I smiled. "You're not far wrong." I sipped, watching her. "I hope you're not regretting it. We can move on if you want."

"Are you kidding? I love it. I never saw a group of people hate each other so politely. Is this what Brits are really like, Stone? I thought it was just the movies."

"Some. This small archipelago has a very complex society."

She held my eye a moment, still smiling. "Let's make a bet."

"What kind of bet?"

"Who will the victim be, and who will the killer be. So far I don't think it's the butler."

I laughed, then shrugged and gazed out at the slowly gathering dusk, which the Scots call the gloaming. "The victim is obvious," I said, playing her game for a moment, but feeling oddly uncomfortable about it.

"The old man? CG Sr.?" I nodded and she nodded back. "I agree."

"The murderer . . ." I shook my head. "I have some ideas, but we're here on our honeymoon, and I don't want to tempt the gods . . ."

I trailed off. It was as though the word had some hidden power of evocation. In the sky, over the broken stone wall and the trees in the north, a great plume of green light shot up into the sky, flickered, and spread out like a fan. Dehan saw my face and said, "What?"

I took her hand and pulled her to her feet, then turned her around. A violet arch swelled like a great dome from the horizon, then shimmered and seemed to break up and spread like mist. Next thing the sky had turned green, and long, vertical columns of light, like immensely tall ghosts, sprang up and wavered this way and that. From the center, a plume of red expanded, and within it, light flashed and seemed to move around in some crazy kind of dance. Dehan had gone rigid, gripping my hand as though she were trying to crush the bones. The red plume swelled, rising above the green light until half the sky was awash with eerie, alien light, twisting and flickering like a gossamer curtain over a parallel world of Norse gods and daemons. Then, as quickly as it had appeared, it began to fade.

She turned to face me. Her eyes were huge and bright. She tried to speak, but words cannot express the way you feel the first time you see the Northern Lights. So she expressed it to me a different way.

A footfall behind me made me turn. Dr. Ian Cameron stood framed in the doorway. He studied me a moment and said, "I'm sorry to interrupt. We're going in to dinner, if you'd like to join us."

Like the honeymoon suite, the dining room was exactly what you would have expected from a Hollywood production of

Murder at Castle Gordon. The ceiling was high; the table was long, dark, highly polished, and mahogany, and set with place mats because tablecloths are considered vulgar. Three large silver candelabras were set down the center, and a vast crystal chandelier made tiny rainbows of the candlelight above the table.

Charles Gordon Sr., naturally, sat at the head. Bee—Lady Jane —sat on his right and Sally Cameron on his left. I was next to Bee, with the major opposite me and Pamela on my right, with her son, Gordon Jr., on her right. Dehan was between the major and Ian.

A door opened at the far end of the room and Brown, very dignified in tails, entered carrying a very large tray with a silver soup tureen. Behind him were two girls in uniform with white aprons. They each carried a silver ice bucket with a bottle of white wine in it. I caught Dehan's eye and winked at her. While the butler was serving the soup, and the maids were pouring the wine, Gordon Sr. boomed down the table, "I am an American, Carmen."

She glanced at him. "Boston born and bred, I'd say."

He laughed like a caricature of Orson Wells at his most hammy. "See! She *is* a detective!"

"I just know my accents, Mr. Gordon. Here I'm not a detective. I am a newlywed bride."

His face went sour. "How charming," he said. "I am an American, but this island belonged to my ancestors, along with much of the coast, for at least a thousand years. It was my father who reclaimed it, back in 1980. He was obsessed with his Scottish roots. He used to wear a kilt, you know? I haven't the legs for it."

He sipped his wine and smiled at Sally. She looked away and Bee simpered. "Nonsense, Charles. You have a well-turned leg!"

"How would you know, Bee?" It was Pamela.

Bee affected to think, with her finger on her cheek. "Well, I'm blessed if I know, darling! But am I wrong?"

Everybody laughed except Pamela.

I said, "Have you been here since the eighties, Mr. Gordon?"

"Yes. Since my father, Richard Gordon, died." He stared at me, as though challenging me to ask. I didn't, so he went on, "He committed suicide in his study, almost forty years ago."

"I'm sorry to hear that."

Pamela replied, breaking a hot bread roll. "Not everybody thought it was suicide."

He snapped, "That's quite enough of that, Pamela!"

She ignored him and went on, "Some people thought it was murder."

CHAPTER 3

BY THE END OF THE SOUP, GORDON SR., BEE, AND SALLY had fallen into conversation with each other. I couldn't help feeling grateful. Ian and Pam maintained their characteristic sullen silence throughout, and Dehan, the major, and I fell into conversation about the history of the island.

"It was," the major said, "for a long time merely a glorified pig farm! Hence the name Swona. It derives from 'swine.' Keeping them on an island was safer than a farm, easier to protect and impossible for the animals to stray."

Dehan asked, "How old is the castle?"

"There has been a small fortress here since the Vikings, first intended to fend them off, and then used by them to protect their settlements. The swine were a highly prized asset, as you can imagine."

We had been served lamb cutlets with new potatoes, Vichy carrots and fresh garden peas, all from the castle's own orchards. Dehan was engrossed in her food but looked up to ask, "So when did it come into the possession of the Gordons?"

"Oh." He sipped his claret and smacked his lips. "The earliest record of a Gordon owning the island dates back to the thirteenth century. In the parish record it is stated that it was a dispute settled by contest of arms, which was won by one Charles Gordon, who fatally wounded his opponent with a blow to the head, thus rendering the estate his in lieu of monies due."

"They didn't mess around in those days, huh, Major?"

"Quite so. It remained then in the Gordon family for almost seven hundred years, until the eighteenth century, when they were overtaken by several misfortunes, not least an attack of swine fever, which wiped out the pigs on the island and ruined the family. Charles Sr.'s great-grandfather, six times over, if you follow me, sold what little possessions he had left and sailed for Boston in 1780 or thereabouts, but it wasn't until the great drive east, after the Civil War, that Charles, Richard Gordon, began to amass his fortune. He never left Boston, but he invested in cattle farms, mining, gun trafficking . . . you name it! And by the turn of the century, he was one of the richest men in Boston."

We had finished our main course, except for Dehan, who was picking up the bones and nibbling at them. She caught a glance from Pam and said, "It's finger food, right?"

Pam looked away and Brown and the maids started clearing the table. Ian got to his feet and spoke loudly over Gordon Sr.'s conversation, forcing him and Sally and Bee to turn and look. His accent seemed to have grown stronger with the wine.

"Ut's late. We need ta be gone. C'mon, Sally, git yer thungs."

Sally turned to him with narrowed eyes.

Gordon Sr. boomed, "You have not even finished your meal, man! Can't you at least wait for coffee?"

Ian's face hardened. "No. We're gone now. But thanks for a wonderful evening, *Charles*!"

Just for a moment I saw savagery and hatred in his face. Sally sighed, stood, and flounced out of the room. Ian looked at us all as though he knew some shocking truth about us and said, "I'll wish yiz all a good evening!" Then he left, trailing his self-conscious dignity.

After he had gone, Pam stood too. "Actually, I'm quite tired myself. I think I'll turn in." She did something with her mouth that could not be bothered to be a smile and added, "Night, all," and followed Ian out of the room.

Gordon Sr. heaved a big sigh and threw his napkin on the table. "Fine!" he said gracelessly. "If there is to be no entertainment, and my wife is not to attend me, then I too shall bid you all a good night and retire." He stood and stared at Dehan. "I breakfast and lunch in my chambers, but I shall no doubt see you at dinner tomorrow. Unless of course you care to pay me a visit." He paused deliberately for a long second, then turned to me, as though pretending to include me in the invitation.

I held his eye. "Good night, Mr. Gordon."

Unlike Ian, he gathered his dignity about him like robes of office and left the room.

Charles Gordon Jr. expostulated breathlessly, "Well!" Then he stammered, "We, we, um, we're left with our cozy little group then! And, and, and . . . *that's* nice! Who's for sticky toffee pudding?"

We had sticky toffee pudding, which was astonishingly good, and then withdrew to the withdrawing room to have coffee and whiskey, though Bee had cognac. We settled ourselves by the fire, the major, Dehan, and myself, armed with generous measures of single malt, while Charles and Bee took their drinks to a small card table near the French windows and played canasta together.

The major smiled happily, sipped, smacked his lips, and sighed. I looked at Dehan. She was examining her drink, and I was wondering how long it would take her to ask. It didn't take long. She raised her eyes to the major and said, "What did Mrs. Gordon mean when she said some people thought Richard Gordon had been murdered?"

He gave a small, comfortable chuckle. "Couldn't resist it, hey? Well, it was all rather peculiar, to tell the truth. Long time ago now, 1981, I suppose. Old Man Gordon, that's Charles Jr.'s grandfather, hadn't long bought the castle. His family were very rich, of course, having made their fortune in the previous century. But his passion, as I told you before, was to return to his roots and reclaim the land that he felt belonged to him and his family by right. When his wife died . . ." He paused, frowning at the fire, and mumbled half to himself, "Never really sure actually if she died or they divorced, but that's neither here nor there, really . . ." He looked back at Dehan and raised his eyebrows. "That's exactly what he did."

I sipped. "So he bought it in 1980."

"That's right. Of course, Charles Sr. was only in his early twenties at the time, finishing at university in Boston. He read law, or as you would say, he majored in law, and came out to join his father when he graduated, which must have been '81 or '82, I suppose. And what he found was a rather peculiar setup."

Dehan arched her eyebrows. "Peculiar in what way?"

"Well, for a start, it seemed that Old Man Gordon was going a bit . . . odd! He had started researching all the families that lived on the island, looking into their family backgrounds, finding out how long they had lived here and, above all, if any of them were related to him. It became something of an obsession."

I frowned. "Aren't most people in communities like this related to each other?"

He spread his hands. "Well, exactly! But he found one family, the Armstrongs, who were in fact quite closely related, via the mother, who was in fact a Gordon. And he sort of *adopted* this family."

"Adopted them?"

He nodded down at his glass. "To the extent that he was considering putting young Robert Armstrong into his will. As you can imagine, Charles Sr., when he arrived at his new home from university in Boston, was quite alarmed at the situation. His father was talking about 'raising up' the Gordons once more and 're-empowering' them. He wanted to reunite the clan . . ." He shook his head. "All sorts of mad stuff. He had clearly lost the plot, as they say these days, and Charles was understandably worried, as he could see his family's considerable fortune being squandered on some bizarre project and, frankly, pilfered by unscrupulous people claiming to be related to him."

Dehan shifted in her seat. "So, what happened?"

The major sighed. "Well, at first not very much . . . Charles begged his father to reconsider his relationship with the Armstrongs, and to put some kind of financial cap on his so-called project, but his father wouldn't hear of it. He continued to restore the castle . . ." He waved his hand around. "Forty years ago this was largely a ruin. He restored it and refurnished it with genuine antiques. That, at least, was an investment. But his increasing closeness with young Robert Armstrong, and the vast amounts of money he was spending on him and his mother, that was cause for genuine concern." He paused, tipping his glass this way and that. "Then things got much more complicated."

I raised an eyebrow and smiled. "More?"

"Yes, because Charles Gordon Sr. fell in love."

"Let me guess," I said. "He fell in love with a girl who was of the wrong social class."

The major looked a little startled.

I smiled. "I may be an American, Major, but I lived here long enough to learn to distinguish the accents. I know a non-U accent when I hear one. Even if it's been disguised."

"Oh!" He stammered a moment. "Well, yes, that was precisely it. She was the daughter of the local publican. Very attractive young woman with a very lively personality. Had a sort of saucy wit, if you follow me. And young Charles was quite captivated by her. Absolutely head over heels."

Dehan was watching him with narrowed eyes. "This is . . ." She pointed vaguely in the direction of the dining room.

He nodded. "Pam, yes." He nodded again. "Well, as you can imagine, Old Man Gordon disapproved violently of the match. He might be sponsoring Robert Armstrong, whom many would consider inappropriate, but at least he was related to the Gordons. But this girl, however delightful she might be, was neither a Gordon nor an appropriate spouse for a Gordon!"

Dehan both frowned and smiled at the same time. "I think I know where this is going."

The major chuckled. "Don't be too quick, Detective. It isn't as simple as it seems. Nobody knows exactly what happened because Charles Sr. won't discuss it, but one version of the story goes something like this:

"Things came to a head when Old Man Gordon told Charles that if he persisted in his plans to marry Pamela, he would disinherit him and leave his entire fortune to Robert Armstrong. Charles agonized for a full week. He told Pamela he could not see her, and he spent seven days either walking the grounds or locked in his room, brooding. Finally, on the seventh day, he went and spoke to his father. They spent over an hour discussing the issue, and when Charles came out he was a different man. He was elated. He ran to the kitchen and embraced the cook and the butler *and* the maids—remember, he was an American—and then he dashed off to tell Pam his father had had a change of heart! It was as though a cloud had been lifted from his mind and he had come down to Earth to realize the error of his ways. He gave Charles his blessing to marry whomever he pleased, and he told Charles he would kill the project and contact his brokers immediately to start reinvesting in solid stocks and shares, as he had done for most of his adult life."

"That's quite a turnaround."

The major nodded. "It is. It's not unheard of, but it was dramatic. And I need hardly say, a huge relief for the entire household."

I nodded. "I can imagine. So, what happened?"

"Well." He sat forward. "That's where it began to get very strange indeed. Refill?"

He went away and came back with the decanter. He refilled our glasses and settled back in his chair.

"As I said, Charles had gone straightaway to see Pam and tell her the good news. When he'd returned a couple of hours later, he went to see his father, planning to tell him that he and Pam had set a date. He knocked on the door . . ."

Dehan interrupted. "What door?"

"Of his study, across the hall, in the tower. He knocked, but there was no reply. When he tried to open the door, he found it locked. This in itself was not unusual, he tended to lock himself in his study when he was working. But he failed to answer when Charles knocked and called to him, despite the fact that, through the window, as he had arrived back home, Charles had seen his father sitting at his desk.

"Concerned that he might be ill, he kicked at the lock several times until he broke it . . ." He paused and shook his head, gazing at the flames in the fire. "It defied belief. Old Man Gordon was sitting at his desk with a bullet wound in his right temple, and his .38 service revolver lying on the floor beside him. All the windows were locked on the inside, as had been the door."

I frowned. "He committed suicide."

The major nodded several times. "That would be the logical conclusion, and it was what the coroner concluded in the end. But the detective who conducted the initial inquiry was never satisfied. Chap from Scotland Yard, came up because of the high profile of the deceased, and because Charles was convinced from the beginning that something was wrong, and frankly, we haven't got the forensic know-how up here to deal with a complex case."

Dehan asked, "What was it that didn't satisfy them?"

"Well, you must remember that in the 1980s, forensic science was still in its infancy, but this chap, Inspector Henry Green, he thought that the angle of the shot was all wrong. If you shoot yourself in the head, the entry wound should be horizontal, and there should be a great deal of scorching because the muzzle is actually touching the head. But in this case, though his prints were all over the gun, the entry wound was at a slight, forty-five-degree angle, and there was no scorching, as though he had held the gun at a distance, and at the height of his hip, which would clearly be impossible. There was also the issue of gunshot residue."

"What about it?"

"There was none on his hand."

I frowned and studied my whiskey for a moment. "So the inference was that he had been shot from a sitting or squatting position, at a distance."

"That's right, but it was clearly impossible because, as I say, the windows were all locked from the inside, as was the door. Charles, as I said, had had to smash the lock when he went in."

Dehan looked at me, frowning and smiling at the same time. "Son of a gun!" She looked back at the major. "And the cops confirmed that the door had been locked . . ."

"Oh yes, you could see very clearly where the latch had burst through the wood."

I said, "You were there?"

He nodded. "I was a friend of the family at the time, part-time PA to Old Man Gordon. There was no question but that the door had been locked from the inside."

I smiled. "Secret passages? Secret doors . . . ?"

"Not uncommon in these old castles, at all. But the police searched high and low and there was nothing. Two walls give onto the outside, a third onto the entrance hall, and the fourth gives onto the ballroom."

Dehan gave a little laugh. "A true locked-room mystery, whad-d'ya know?" Then she laughed out loud. "This isn't something you lay on especially for American detective guests?"

He chuckled. "A police variation on the Canterville Ghost! No, no! I'm afraid not. That is exactly how it happened. You can read it in the John o'Groats local papers. It also made the national press, briefly. You can probably find the papers in the library." He pointed behind him at a door in the paneled wall. "Through that door."

Dehan grinned. "I might have a look tomorrow."

I raised an eyebrow at her, then smiled at the major. "We run a cold-cases unit in New York. We specialize in unsolved homicides." I looked back at Dehan, who was still grinning. "But we're supposed to be on honeymoon, remember?"

The major laughed. "Oh dear! I should have kept quiet, shouldn't I?" Then he shrugged. "But of course, strictly, this is *not* a cold case. It was closed, as a suicide."

Dehan made a face. "And that's probably what it was. The absence of GSR and burns may have a perfectly simple explanation. Easier to explain that than how the killer got out of a locked room."

"And an explanation," I said, setting down my glass, "that *we* are not going to provide." I stood. "Come along, Mrs. Stone. I am dead beat."

And we went up, arm in arm, to our ancient, Scottish bedchamber.

Scan the QR code below to purchase MURDER MOST SCOTTISH.
Or go to: righthouse.com/murder-most-scottish